D0889737

The Women
in Her Dreams

A Novel by

Candace Denning

NORTH POINT PRESS
San Francisco 1988

I want to thank Robert Lescher, Jack Shoemaker, and
William Turnbull for having faith.

And for their support, my thanks to The MacDowell
Colony, the Virginia Center for the Creative Arts, and
the Virginia Commission for the Arts.

This book is also dedicated to my great-grandmother
Lillian Trexler Howell from whose journal I borrowed.

For Sandy

I.

One

Sarah Broderhouse walked toward her twin sister and the river with the feeling that she was walking toward the woman in her dream. Her sister was standing on a ferry landing in a wedding dress. It was a cloudy September day in central Illinois. It was 1969.

"Here she comes," a man shouted. He was standing outside his car on the ramp. The woman inside stared out.

Sarah carried camera equipment. She was the photographer and Laura was the bride.

Laura asked, "Have you ever noticed the way women in beehive hairdos look unhappy?" She watched the man drive the woman onto the ferry. "She probably didn't want to marry him. Thirty years later she finds herself trapped inside a car on a ferry. Outside is this girl in a wedding dress."

The ferryman pulled a heavy chain across the back of the ferry. The ferry began to move away from the dock.

"You don't have to marry Matthew if you don't want to," Sarah said. She tore open a roll of film and loaded her camera.

"Don't you think we make a neat couple?" Laura asked.

"You go well together," Sarah said. Their contrast was good. Matthew was blond and Laura was brunette.

"We're a team," Laura said in her dreamy voice.

Sarah took a close-up. The ferry sounded its horn in the distance. The river was not wide.

"It isn't too late to get out of it," she said. She felt pent up inside. "It's never too late."

"Yes it is," Laura said and hid her hands behind her neck. "Matthew's friends are coming out from Colorado. And Stanley's flying up."

"Oh Stanley," Sarah said. She'd spent a night with Stanley wrestling on a Murphy bed. If she wasn't going to do it, he wanted to know, why had she gotten into bed with him in the first place?

"Last week I dreamed I was shot," Laura said. She looked peeved. "The bullets went in under the skin in a circle around my heart. No one would remove them. I thought I was going to die and when I didn't, I lost interest."

Laura was a nurse. She worked in the emergency room at the county hospital. She looked at the sky.

"Is it going to rain?" She posed. "It looks like rain."

Sarah took a step back and brought her sister into focus. "It isn't going to rain," she said.

"I felt a drop," Laura said with a frown.

The shutter clicked open and shut.

"I don't think I'm making a mistake," Laura said.

"I didn't say you were," Sarah said.

"You implied it."

"Relax your shoulders," said Sarah. "Try to look friendly." She kept her eye hard against the camera.

"I have something to ask you," Laura said. She touched the corner of her mouth. "The man you met up at the lake this summer was married, wasn't he."

His room was cold and beige like hers, except there was no typewriter on the table as Sarah had expected. They met in the elevator. He looked strong. He said he was a poet.

Sarah didn't want to but she said, "He told me he was separated."

Fat women in lavender stretch tops roamed the boardwalk. The smell of french fries hung in the air and the wrong taste was on her tongue. He said he was looking for the right woman. She tried to be that woman.

"But you know how men are," Laura said.

They went to a lounge where she would normally not set foot and listened to Otis Redding and drank cuba libres. The place was beside the restaurant of a cheap motel. She sank into the vinyl cushions of their booth in the darkest corner and watched women go to and from the ladies' room at the end of the bar. He got up to play pool. She listened to the crack of balls.

"Didn't you stop to consider how his wife might feel?" Laura asked.

"His wife walked in on us," Sarah said.

Laura gasped lightly, like a fish. Sarah took a picture. Nothing that bad had ever happened to Laura.

When his wife opened the closet door, Sarah was standing there wrapped in a sheet. As a twin there was little in life she had been singled out for.

"I thought I was special," his wife said. "Jack?"

"Jesus Christ Brenda," he said getting out of bed. He pulled up his undershorts. "Why didn't you tell me you were coming?"

"He taught me to play pool," said Sarah. "We hustled a few games."

"My God," Laura whispered. She looked into the camera lens. "Didn't you think it was wrong?"

"I didn't think about it," Sarah said.

"How could you not think about it?"

Sarah watched the daylight change. He was the first man she had ever slept with. She adjusted her f-stop. "When you make love to me," she told Jack without shame, "I know I exist."

"Couldn't you have restrained yourself?" Laura asked.

"It wasn't a question of restraint," said Sarah.

Laura pressed her lips together and looked slim. "I just don't want to see you get hurt," she said.

"Is that it," said Sarah.

"Do you ever hear from him?" Laura asked.

If Laura knew the truth, she would tell.

"No, I never do," Sarah said. He had called her from

different towns. Milwaukee, Hammond. Each time she planned to hang up as soon as she heard his voice, then she couldn't. He told her what she was thinking. He warned her she was going to ruin her life.

"I have one more question and then I won't say anything more about it," Laura said. "Were you attracted to him because he was married?"

"I didn't know at first that he was married," Sarah said in a calm voice. When she found out, she whispered *I'm having an affair with a married man*. It was something no one else that she knew was having.

"Did I hear somebody's getting married?" Marvin asked. A Stroh's sign blinked off and on behind him. Marvin also sold bait and fishing supplies.

"In a week," said Laura. They sat at the bar. Marvin's right hand lay on the bar. It only had three fingers.

"Nice guy?" he said.

"Yes, he is," said Laura.

"Why do earthworms come out when it rains?" Sarah asked.

Marvin sold worms. He grinned at her but not in a friendly way.

"I guess it's so they won't drown," she said.

Marvin got two beers out of the cooler and set them on the bar in front of two men dressed as fishermen.

"This place gives me the creeps," Sarah said.

"It's okay," said Laura. "Marvin knows Dad."

She got off the bar stool and walked over to the jukebox. Glen Campbell's voice came out as soon as she put in a quarter. She moved back toward the bar in the late afternoon. Behind her was a red Formica-topped table and the cracked linoleum floor.

"You girls twins?" one of the fishermen asked. "My buddy and me was wondering."

"We're identical twins," Laura said, getting back up on the stool.

"I bet you fool a lot of people," the fisherman said shoving back his cap.

"Being twins is a lot of fun," said Laura.

"I wanted a twin when I was a kid," the other man said. He leaned forward to get a look at them.

Sarah looked back at him. "Everybody says that," she said. "It's because you were lonely." When she was eight, she felt so lonely she invented a secret friend.

"Say. When does this place liven up?" the first man asked.

"A band comes in on Saturday night," Laura said.

"You going to be here Saturday night?" he asked.

"I'm getting married on Saturday," Laura said.

"You're too young to get married," he said. He shook his head and laughed.

"No we're not," Laura said quickly. "We graduated from college in June."

"You went to the university here in town?" he asked.

"Yes, we did," Laura said. She looked at Marvin. "I'm hungry," she said. "Do you have any Polish sausage?"

"You both want one?" Marvin asked.

"I'll give her a Polish sausage," one of the fishermen said.

"Did I say something wrong?" Laura whispered.

Sarah stared at the lava lamp by the cash register in disbelief. She had been a waitress but she didn't think of herself as a waitress. She had slept with a married man but she didn't think of herself as that kind of person either. Laura wouldn't have done those things. Who was right? Sarah looked at Laura in the mirror. Beside her she saw herself caught in someone else's dream.

"Who are you girls anyway?" the fisherman asked.

"We're twin sisters having a beer," Laura said. She hung her arm around Sarah as if they had both just come home.

Laura had been missing for a year. That is, she had abandoned Sarah for Matthew Rand. Freedom from Laura felt bloated and wobbly, like an escaped balloon. Sarah had seen herself rising, her stretched face, her hands floating away.

Two

The woman in Sarah's dream had eyes in the back of her neck, azure eyes. She was walking along a street in a small midwestern town. She passed a white frame house with louvered windows. A black cat in the yard lifted one paw over a broken flower and turned white. Her mother walked on as a cat without a flaw in its stride, over the broken cement beyond a maple dangling clumps of winged seeds toward the earth. The tree's sap seemed about to break and run. The azure cat eyes didn't blink and saw everything.

"It's Sarah," she called.

She stood on the wide front porch of her great-aunts' house. Behind her the street was quiet. The house hadn't always been kept so dark. She pulled the screen door open and stepped into the cool foyer. The air smelled of earth, and somewhere a motor hummed in tune with the pitch of silence ringing through the rooms. The house gave out creaks and sighs, tenants of the dark.

"I know which one you are," Mildred cried from the parlor. Her voice was broken and rich. She was the musical one.

Mildred moved forward and back in her rocker by the piano. Her hands lay asleep on her lap. Sarah sat on the piano stool. Lace curtains veiled the windows making the room dim. She saw herself in front of the windows, backlit and moody.

"Aren't you going to Laura's wedding on Saturday?" she asked.

"Margaret doesn't do as well in crowds as she used to," Mildred said. Her sister Margaret was three years older than she.

"You could go by yourself."

"I don't believe I would," Mildred said. She pulled her knitting from a basket beside the chair. "Where are they going on their honeymoon?"

"To the Bahamas," said Sarah.

"I went to the Rocky Mountains once," said Mildred. She squinted at her knitting. "I opened some French doors and there they were spread out before me."

"I've never been west of the Mississippi," Sarah said. She turned around on the piano stool and played an E-minor scale. An oval picture of Jesus hung above the piano.

"My mother's brother traveled all over Missouri," said Mildred. "He played the trombone and put on shows."

Then Margaret entered the parlor with her shoulders

squared and her cane stuck out. She wore a flowered dress like Mildred's but a size larger. They ordered everything alike from the Montgomery Ward catalogue. Everybody took it for granted that Margaret would live the longest. She took care of the money.

"She was asking if we're going to the wedding," Mildred said and stopped knitting.

"Laura's young man looks like a gentleman," Margaret said.

"Matthew tends to look that way," Sarah said to the keyboard. Matthew was a city boy who wore cowboy boots with his business suits and drove a new yellow truck.

"I don't do as well in crowds as I used to," said Margaret.

"Matthew, Mark, Luke, and John are all nice names," said Mildred.

Margaret walked over to a window and touched the leaves of an African violet. "I believe these plants need water," she said.

From the kitchen Sarah heard the grandfather clock ticking in the library, a cold room. The sound was tentative. She got the watering can from the broom closet and set it in the sink. Suddenly lonely, she turned the faucet on full force and filled the can to overflowing.

"To your right," Margaret was saying as Sarah walked back into the parlor. Mildred was down on her hands and knees patting the carpet with determination.

"Your right," said Margaret. "She doesn't know her right from her left yet. Is it still ticking?"

"Nobody in this family knows their right from their left," said Mildred.

"For heaven's sake," Sarah said. "Get up." She helped Mildred to her feet. "What do you think you're doing?"

"She dropped her watch," Mildred said dusting her bosom.

"I've got to take my watch to Mr. Ogleby for a new band," Margaret said with her pinched look. "Mr. Ogleby carries the bands I like."

"It's Mr. Ogleby you like," said Mildred.

"I'll drive you to Mr. Ogleby's," Sarah said.

"You don't have time," Margaret said. She put the watch in her pocket.

"Yes I do. I'm on my lunch hour," Sarah said. She worked for the newspaper.

"If she wants to do it, let her," said Mildred.

"Some people do things for you and then resent you," Margaret said not looking at them.

"Does everybody have a purse and sweater," Sarah asked in her mother's voice. The voice seemed to come from near the windows.

"I imagine you're worried about riding in this little car," Margaret said in the front seat. Mildred sat in back.

"I'm not worried," said Mildred.

Sarah started the engine. Beyond the shaded street the day was sunny.

"I was a good driver," Margaret said to the windshield. She'd given up driving when she was eighty-three. Mildred never had learned how.

"Can you turn on the heater, dear?" Mildred asked.

"It's not that cold, Aunt Mildred," said Sarah. She tapped the accelerator.

"I feel a chill," said Mildred. "You forgot to water the plants, Margaret."

"I knew we forgot something," Margaret said. She refolded the sweater on her lap.

"Did you turn off the stove?" Mildred asked.

"It's the refrigerator I worry about catching fire."

"If it worries you," Sarah said, "ask Dad to come over and take a look at it." She turned on the heater and pulled away from the curb.

"Lloyd can fix anything," Mildred said. "I'm convinced of that." She made sure her window was rolled up tight.

"I read something in the 'Handyman's Column' about refrigeration coils," Margaret said.

"Did you see the article about the eclipse next spring?" Mildred asked. "It is to be the last major eclipse of the century."

"Well no," said Margaret.

Sarah turned the corner and drove into the sunlight.

"Eclipse means an overshadowing or a dimming," Mildred said. "Even extinction. I looked it up in the dictionary when you girls were born."

A solar eclipse occurred on May 20, 1947, the day Sarah and Laura were born. A UPI story from Bocayuva, Brazil, appeared in the column next to their birth announcement. Everybody remembered it because Uncle Oscar had gone to Brazil in the thirties and never came back.

"An eclipse won't hurt you," Mildred said. "Unless you look right at it."

Three

A horse coughed as they entered the cool barn and Sarah heard flapping overhead. A white horse was tied outside one of the stalls. She took a picture of the light coming down in slats through the roof. She took a picture of the horse.

"The first step is to let them down," Roy Thomas said. "They come off the track high."

"How do you let them down?" she asked, getting out a pencil. He had the face of a boy.

He said, "Let them eat grass for a month. Then start them walking."

She looked at the buckets and sponges and wheelbarrow, the ladder leading to the loft. She looked inside the neat tack room. She smelled it. Roy took a bridle from a nail on the wall and they went back outside. He walked in his cowboy boots like a tall man might walk over new grass.

"You look too young to own your own business," she said. They were moving toward two horses attached to a machine with long metal arms. The horses walked around and around it. They had on western saddles and green halters.

"I've been working since I was seven years old," Roy said. He stopped the walker and bridled the gray horse. It had spots on its rump. The brown one lifted a rear foot.

"I can't imagine working since I was seven," Sarah said in a breathless voice. "My mother said she wanted us to enjoy our childhood."

"Did you enjoy it?" Roy asked.

"A tall carpenter came to our farm the day my sister and I started school," she said. "Why are you going to school? he asked. Because I am ignorant, I said."

Roy didn't smile.

"After we learned to read, my twin sister and I were promoted into the bluebird reading group. I believed it was because we were cute and identical, not because we read well."

"You mean there's another one like you?" Roy said.

She always told people she was a twin. Alone, she felt as if she weren't enough.

She said, "We practiced getting under our desks in case of an air raid. One day Sonny Simpson got stuck. He was terribly fat as a kid. He is still fat. Our teacher had to call the janitor to get him unstuck."

Roy stared at her.

"My sister is getting married on Saturday," she said.

He led the spotted horse into the exercise ring and got on. The horse started trotting around the ring. Sarah sat on the fence. Roy showed her the difference between the jog and lope and demonstrated how to change leads, shouting as he rode. She took pictures.

"Want to give it a try?" he called, coming back over to the fence.

Sarah saw herself riding around the ring as he had, only better. Her father had once owned two horses.

Roy dismounted. "Let me give you a leg up." He looked at her feet. "You should never ride in sneakers but I'll let you this time." He made a stirrup with his hands and hoisted her up.

The ground seemed far away. Sarah held on to the saddle horn.

"Nudge her with your heels. Don't kick. She's still high. Keep your heels down," Roy said.

Sitting in a saddle was uncomfortable.

"Get those heels down," he shouted as the horse walked away.

She hated to be yelled at. Something pinched her calf.

"Don't pull up on the reins. Pull back gently."

The horse wouldn't stop. The horse was going to trot. Now the saddle was slapping her bottom.

"You've got her in a nice jog," Roy shouted.

Sarah tried to laugh but horseback riding was torture. She lost her right stirrup and bent forward to see where it had gone.

"Whoa," she heard Roy say. "Whoa. Oh shit."

Sarah smelled sawdust as she fell forward. Her shoulder hit the ground. She felt violently hungry.

Roy's hand pushed her hair away from her eyes.

"Thank you," she said trying to sit up but he wouldn't let her. She licked her lips and tasted dirt.

"I wasn't expecting a pretty lady," he said looking troubled. "I thought they would send someone old. You know?"

The sun was warm on her cheek, on her neck. The day had grown small.

"Would you like a glass of water?" he asked.

"A glass of water," she said.

He leaned over her. She felt his breath on her mouth. "I'd better get you into the house," he said.

"My shoulder hurts," she said.

"Up you go," he said lifting her. "It's good to fall off a horse every once in a while so you know it won't kill you."

She wondered if she was too heavy for him. He was so thin.

"I fall off all the time," he said.

He carried her through his kitchen, down a dim hallway, into a small bedroom. In it were a child's bed and a child's chair. She knew it was ridiculous but she let him put her on the bed. The sheets smelled clean. Her hand lay on the cool pillow. Her hand looked as if it never held anything heavier than water or light, the way her mother's hand looked. Sarah felt like her mother's hand. She lay on her stomach and let Roy rub her back. He pulled up her shirt and touched her skin.

"You have a beautiful back," he said. "I love your bones." He unfastened her bra and kissed her spine in three places.

She saw no way to stop him. She felt sleepy and rolled over. He fingered one nipple. His tongue moved slowly across her lower lip. His tongue moved gently around her nipple.

"I have to ask you some questions," she said barely speaking.

In the late afternoon he moved his mouth down her belly. He kissed her pelvic bones. She took a deep breath. He looked up at her but he didn't smile. She saw her mother's eyes staring at her through a rearview mirror.

"Do you trade horses?" she asked. "Do you break them?"

Four

All at once the sun seemed too hot hanging over the church at noon. Sarah stood still and watched the truck begin to move.

"Run," Laura shouted.

She and Matthew sat on aluminum lawn chairs in the back of his yellow pickup. Matthew's brother Bruce stood behind them in a rented tuxedo with one hand on Matthew's shoulder as in a family portrait. Sarah chased the truck. The shoe factory whistle went off. Somebody laughed. It hurt. She was the missing person, the twin sister of the bride, and the bride was stealing the men.

"Way to go," Matthew's brother said giving her his hand. He pulled her up onto the tailgate.

"Stanley did that on purpose," she said. Stanley was

driving. Since the night in the Murphy bed, she believed he found her ridiculous.

Bruce put his arm around her. He was two years younger. "At least he didn't run over your foot," he said.

Sarah pressed her cheek against the slick lapel of his jacket. She was with him at the A&W the night some clown backed over his foot. He yelled motherfuck, pardon my French, and hopped around outside her car. She didn't know what to do so she drove him to her parents' house. Bruce didn't want to go to the hospital she explained as her father put on shoes. Had anyone gotten the license plate number? Of course not. Lloyd was exasperated. It was the middle of the night.

"Hang on to the back of that chair," the orderly told Lloyd in the emergency room. "These old wooden ones are so tall they tip right over." Lloyd held the wheelchair as Bruce sat down in it. Bruce leaned forward to remove his sock and Lloyd let go. Sarah knew immediately her father had done it on purpose. The wheelchair was on top of Bruce.

"Dad gum it. I'm sorry," Lloyd said.

The truck careened around a corner and went fast up a shaded side street. It stopped in front of their great-aunts' house. Everybody stayed in the truck. Matthew put his tanned face next to Laura's as if they were having their picture taken. They laughed and waved.

"Doesn't everybody look pretty," Mildred cried waving back. She and Margaret sat dressed up on the porch swing.

"We love you," Laura called.

The porch was framed by lattice covered with vines. The

vines had been there so long, they held up the lattice now. The two old ladies stayed on the porch swing. Nothing in the picture moved except the swing, which moved only slightly.

"Was it a nice wedding?" Mildred asked as Margaret buttoned her sweater.

"It was beautiful," Laura said. "Somebody painted HELP on the soles of Matthew's shoes."

"We should have had someone drive them to the wedding," Laura said as the truck pulled away. "Why didn't we?"

"If they had wanted to come, they would have found a way," said Matthew.

"No. It was my fault," Laura said with regret.

"Old people are much happier at home," Matthew said.

"We should have gotten out of the truck at least," Laura said. "We should have gone up onto the porch instead of screaming at them from the street."

"How much longer are we going to discuss this?" Matthew asked with irritation.

An old red Cadillac with fins drove up behind them. Sarah took pictures of the Cadillac with four arms sticking out the windows. They were Stockman arms. The Stockmans were her mother's side of the family. The Cadillac followed them honking through town. Conversation was impossible.

Seven miles out into the country they turned off the highway onto a county road. Gravel pinged the belly of the truck. The air smelled dusty. In the flat distance the Stockman homestead stood lonely in the fields, connected to the outside world only by power and telephone lines.

The pickup swerved into the yard and parked under a live oak. "Is your phone out again?" a cousin asked somebody. Bruce jumped to the ground. He put his hands around Sarah's waist and lifted her down through the warm afternoon. "Oooooo," the cousin said. "What a gorgeous dress Laura has on."

Sarah and Laura wore identical linen dresses except that Laura's was eggshell and Sarah's was celery. When they were kids, they insisted on dressing alike and wearing their hair the same. Only Laura wore glasses.

"It's ridiculous in this day and age when a man can get to the moon but he can't get through on his own telephone," somebody said.

"Rural phones are out of order an average of eight to ten days a month," Sarah said with a cardboard feeling.

Inside the old brick house was dim and cool. Laura stood in the sunlight by the stairway. She stood still and looked lovely.

"What are you thinking?" Sarah asked.

"Nothing," said Laura.

"You look nervous," Sarah said. She knew it was a cruel thing to say.

"Well I'm not," said Laura.

They walked into the dining room and Laura surveyed the buffet. Sarah picked up a piece of cauliflower and stuck it into a lumpy dip. The lumps were blue cheese. Their father walked up and began sorting through the broccoli. He was not a tall man. None of the Broderhouse men was tall.

"You look great in your tux, Dad," said Laura.

Lloyd patted his stomach. He'd lost weight for the wedding. "This is real nice," he said.

"Thanks for everything Dad."

"Are you happy Sister?" he asked.

Laura started to cry.

"It isn't anything to cry about," he said digging in his back pocket. "Here take my handkerchief."

Matthew's father came over and put his arm around Laura. "We're real happy to get this little girl in our family," he said. Laura stood still and said nothing. Harold Rand was in heating and air conditioning.

"Tell your boy he better take care of her," said Lloyd.

"Say Lloyd," said Harold. "I've been wondering how you locate your wells." He glanced behind Lloyd.

"I witch them with a coat hanger," said Lloyd.

"I'll be a son-of-a-gun," said Harold. He laughed uproariously. "Ever tried a peach branch?"

"You can't always find a peach branch," Lloyd said. "If you know what I mean. But there's usually a hanger around somewhere."

"Did you hear about the guy who locates water in South America by concentrating on a map?" Harold asked in his loud voice. "He never sets foot there."

"Some people can do it," Lloyd seemed to shout back.

"Do you know where your sister is going on her honeymoon?" he asked after Harold had taken Laura away.

"No Dad," Sarah said.

"Did I ever tell you about the shivaree my dad pulled when his cousin got married?"

"About a hundred times, Dad."

"Albert and Birdie took the train to St. Louis for their honeymoon. By the time they got to the hotel, he'd already been there." Lloyd grinned. His father had set white mice loose in their room.

"I guess things were funnier back then," said Sarah.

"Do you remember that, Mother?" Lloyd asked.

Myrtie Broderhouse had wandered over with a champagne glass full of ginger ale. She thought everyone was drinking ginger ale.

"I remember it," she said in her singsong voice.

"Shivarees are a thing of the past, Dad," said Sarah. She reached around him for a cherry tomato. "It would be torture not to be able to get away from your family if you really wanted to." She thought Albert, Birdie, and Myrtie sounded like names that belonged to a certain type of people. When she was with them she wanted to open windows, repaint the rooms.

"I'd like some real food," Lloyd said looking around. "Not that this isn't nice."

Sarah looked at her father and felt like crying. She understood his hunger. She put her arms around him and hugged him.

"What was that for?" he asked hugging her back.

"I don't know," said Sarah.

"This is a big day for your sister," he said. "That boy should do all right."

Matthew had come down from Chicago to college when he couldn't get into Northwestern. He stayed on after graduation because he thought he could make a killing in real estate.

"I imagine he will," said Sarah.

The only one of her boyfriends her parents had liked was

Charles Reed. Charles was six-four and his family owned farms. Charles was so tall, Sarah could never guess what he was thinking. He resembled the men on her mother's side of the family and she tried hard to love him. She knew he was a good person. He bought her expensive perfume. Each time she put it on, she felt like more than herself.

The afternoon Charles walked into their living room, her mother stood up and clasped her hands neatly before her like a bad girl, or a very good girl. Sarah had never seen her mother act this way before. Charles took her mother's hand as if he had been taught to kiss it.

"Sit down, Mother," Sarah thought.

Irene sat in the old leather armchair by the bookcase and Sarah and Charles sat close on the sofa far across the room. Charles did not hold her hand. He leaned forward with his elbows on his knees. Sarah looked at the pictures on the wall of her mother's great-grandfather and great-uncles in stiff white collars. None of them was smiling.

"I like my beef well done too," Charles said.

"When you've seen it on the hoof, you can't stomach it any other way," said Irene.

Thank goodness her mother was serving leg of lamb. Thank goodness she was not going to fix fried chicken.

"If your mother was twenty years younger," her father said that night, "you'd have yourself some competition."

Now, as Lloyd turned away from the buffet wiping his fingers on his handkerchief, he started to say it again.

"If your mother was twenty years younger," he said.

If her mother were twenty years younger, would she

choose a different life? Irene never said she was unhappy but she was always looking for improvement.

"There you are," Irene said coming into the kitchen.

Sarah looked around at the pine cupboards. "I got hungry," she said. She looked at her mother in her peach colored dress. Her mother looked ideal.

"There's plenty of food in the dining room," Irene said like a suggestion.

Sarah remembered a snapshot of her mother on a beach in Delaware. She and Lloyd were newlyweds. She was holding a big hat on her head and smiling as if life had never disappointed her.

"I wanted to be by myself," Sarah said. She picked up a cracker with an anchovy on it. She didn't even like anchovies.

"Is something wrong?" Irene asked.

"I know I'm supposed to be happy for Laura but I'm not," Sarah said.

"Everybody has mixed feelings at weddings," said Irene. "Try to concentrate on the good ones."

"I don't have any good ones," Sarah said. She put the cracker in her mouth. "I don't mean to feel this way. I just do."

"I think you do mean to feel this way sometimes," Irene said in a helpful way. "Don't you ever think so?"

"No I don't," Sarah said.

"I don't want you to go through life miserable like your grandmother," said Irene. "I believe she enjoys feeling miserable."

"Don't you want to know why I feel bad?"

"Not if we're going to stand out here for a long time and discuss it," Irene said. She looked at her watch. "My goodness. Here we are out in the kitchen with a party going on in the other room."

When she was eleven, Sarah tried not to make death wishes but she made them. Several times a day she confessed to her mother. Confessing made her feel safe. At first Irene was forgiving and then she grew distant.

"When Matthew came along," Sarah said, "Laura changed. She grew out her nails and started wearing spike heels."

"You sound jealous, Sarah. I'm ashamed of you," said Irene.

"It's not just me she's left," Sarah said. "She seems to have left herself."

"I think this is normal. Getting married is a big step."

"If this is what happens when you get married, I hope I never get married."

"It breaks my heart to see you this way," Irene said. "I want you girls to be close. You only have one sister." She looked worried. "My sisters and I always meant to go on a vacation together, just the four of us," she said. "But we never did."

"It isn't too late," Sarah said feeling sorry. "You could still go on a vacation."

"We have families to take care of," said Irene. She touched her eye with one finger. "Now. Put a smile on your face and go back out there. This is your sister's wedding."

Sarah wished her mother would hug her. She wanted to

feel forgiven. Her mother left the kitchen. Sarah looked at the brittle wallpaper curling off the wall behind the stove and felt angry. She wanted to feel more joy and pain than Irene would allow. She wanted to have experiences Irene wouldn't dream of.

"You didn't tell Dad where we're going, did you?" Laura asked by the punch bowl.

"Of course not," Sarah said filling her cup with punch.

"Thank you for the beautiful service, Reverend," Laura said.

"I thought this was ginger ale," said the minister's wife. Sarah turned around with her camera ready. "Say cheese," she said.

The minister's wife put a glove over her mouth and Sarah took the picture.

"I just wish Peter could have been here," Laura said. She hung an arm around Sarah.

"Wouldn't that have been nice?" the minister's wife said with sympathy. Peter was their younger brother who had gone off to Canada.

"Matthew loves you too," Laura said to Sarah. "You're his sister now." She smiled at the minister's wife and went away.

"I'm not Matthew's sister," Sarah said to the minister's wife.

"Hey Twinnie," Geraldine Huckleberry called. She came over with a cigarette in front of her and a large flat purse trapped under one arm. She was short but she was built.

"Mrs. Huck," said Sarah. They didn't hug. Geraldine was

their best friend's mother. She walked catlike on the soft, thick soles of her white nurse's shoes. She was nothing like their mother.

"It's your turn next, Twinnie," she said. Geraldine never had been able to tell them apart.

"I'm in no hurry," said Sarah.

"If you had you some four hundred film, you could shoot inside without a flash on a day like this," Uncle Morris said. He looked asleep on his feet. He slipped one hand inside his white shirt and scratched his chest. He had the long, thin Stockman nose.

"I believe you," Sarah said. They had had this conversation before.

"Get ready," said Uncle Morris. "Here they come."

"Here they come," Geraldine whispered on tiptoe.

Laura appeared radiant at the top of the stairs. Laura could appear radiant at will. Matthew stood beside her wearing his grin. They walked down the steps. Sarah watched the air fill with rice like a grainy picture. She listened for the explosion of laughter and applause.

Five

She saw him through the plate-glass window of King's Drugstore. Roy Thomas in his cowboy hat was reading the label on a bottle of aftershave. Sarah didn't want to go into the drugstore but she did. It was Saturday afternoon.

"Hi Roy," she said.

"I'm sorry," he said. He quickly put the bottle back on the shelf.

She told him her name.

"That's right," he said and snapped his fingers.

"I wasn't myself the other day," she said looking at the shelf behind him.

"You took quite a fall," he said and shoved one hand into his jeans pocket.

"I wouldn't want you to think I have that reaction every time I fall off a horse," she said.

"I didn't think that," he said and moved toward her to make room for a woman in the aisle behind him. Sarah reached for a bottle of perfume on the shelf. She sprayed her wrist and held it to her nose. The woman walked behind Roy again.

"Look," he said. "Can I buy you a beer?"

She saw them driving along a bumpy dirt road in his truck. He was taking her someplace she did not want to go. The landscape was flat but it was not Illinois.

She shrugged. "Why not?" she said.

The jukebox was playing when they walked into Marvin's bar. A couple was barely moving on the dance floor. Sarah smelled the sawdust on the floor. She smelled cigar smoke. They moved across the dance floor and sat at a small Formica table near the jukebox.

"I'll get us a pitcher," Roy said.

She watched him walk to the bar. She watched him walk back.

"Everything okay?" he asked. He put the pitcher on the table and sat down.

Sarah poured the beer. "Did you see the photographs I took of your horses?" she asked. "They were in last Saturday's paper." She had printed one of Roy for herself.

"I don't read the paper very often," he said.

"Oh," she said. She looked at the couple on the dance floor.

"I'm sure they were good if you took them," he said.

"My sister got married on Saturday," Sarah said. "Our brother couldn't be there."

"Where was he?" Roy asked.

"Peter quit college and went to Canada last year. He got drafted."

Laura and Peter were playing in the swing below. Sarah watched them through the maple leaves from the attic where she'd been sent to pout. The maple leaves smelled wet. Then it was another day and rain was flooding the gutters. They were allowed to play in the rain, it was so clean. She remembered the sensation of playing naked in the cool rain.

"I've never been out with a college girl before," Roy said.

"You haven't," she said.

"Do you want to dance?"

"Isn't it too early to dance?"

"It's never to early to dance." He touched her hand. "I want to make love to you again," he said.

"You didn't remember my name," she said. She looked at the beer. She looked at the aluminum ashtray.

"I'm terrible on names. Look. Could we go to your place? I have to be careful. I'm trying to get custody of my little boy."

"You're trying to get custody of your little boy?" she said.

"My ex-wife is negligent," he said. "I can prove she isn't a fit mother."

Sarah listened to the Otis Redding song that was playing on the jukebox. She had heard it a hundred times in bars with Jack over the summer.

"You sure are a pretty woman," Roy said.

She held her breath. No one had called her a woman before.

Roy took hold of her arm and turned her around. They were in her kitchen. She closed her eyes. She felt his tongue on her lips. He kissed her neck, her collarbone. They moved through the small living room and started undressing in the hallway. When they got to the bed they were naked. Sarah shoved the books and clothes off onto the floor and they got in between the cool sheets. She lay on her stomach and Roy rubbed her back.

"You have a beautiful back," he said. "I love your bones." He kissed her spine in three places. She rolled over and felt him touch one nipple with his finger. His tongue moved slowly across her lower lip. It moved gently around her nipple. She waited for him to move his mouth down along her ribs. She felt lonely. He was doing everything exactly as before.

"Is it hot in here?" he asked raising his head. "Should I open a window?"

"The windows are painted shut," she said.

He kissed her pelvic bones and she took a deep breath. She didn't even like him but she felt she must let this happen to her.

"What's wrong," he said moving himself between her legs.

"Nothing," she said.

She listened to a car drive by on the street below. She watched the sky through the top of the window. Maybe she was the only girl he made love to in the afternoon.

"Please don't go," she said when he raised himself up on his elbow.

He looked proud. "I have work to do, darlin'," he said. "I have a business to run."

"This is terrible," she said to her bedroom.

"I'll be back," he said. He got out of bed and tucked the sheet around her.

Six

"In His name, our precious Lord and Savior Jesus Christ, we pray," Uncle Veachel said.

Sarah studied the pattern on the water glass in front of her. It was the old family crystal. She wondered who would get it.

"Amen," everybody said and kissed.

Veachel raised his arms as if he were going to direct a hymn. He was Lloyd's older brother. "Can't hear you," he used to shout at the congregation. "Louder for the Lord," he'd say.

"I don't sing anymore because I was forced to as a little boy," Lloyd had told his kids.

When Sarah and Laura were small, their grandmother made them get up in front of her congregation and sing "Jesus Loves Me." Once, they couldn't stop giggling. *Aren't*

*they cute? And so identical. One of them has a mole on her arm.
Which one has the mole?* They practiced Saturday afternoons at her house. Myrtie's piano room was still cold and bare.

"Pass to the left," Veachel said. He put down his arms. He was short but sat tall, an ex-marine.

"I hope those yams aren't too sweet," Aunt Vera said.

"How's your back?" Lloyd asked his sister-in-law, handing her the green beans.

Vera began to describe her back exercises.

"Everybody take some more," Myrtie said.

"You want us all to get fat, don't you," said Irene. Behind her in the china closet were several pieces of carnival glass.

"She's not eating a thing," Myrtie said to Vera.

"Why she is," Vera said interrupting herself. "You're the one who's not eating."

Marianne passed the fried chicken to her husband Bob. Marianne was the only Broderhouse cousin. She and the twins had grown up together.

"Did you hear Karen Blackford had her baby?" Marianne said. She held her heart. "She was in labor for thirty hours."

Sarah had seen Marianne and Bob drive around in their sensible Chevrolet, sitting up straight as if they never talked to each other.

"When I had the boys I didn't feel a thing," Myrtie said. "Doc Hutchins gave me a shot."

"What did he give you, Mother?" Vera asked. She winked at Irene.

"I don't remember the name of it," Myrtie said. "It was some drug."

"Geraldine Huckleberry called yesterday," Sarah said. "Kate had a little girl. You remember Kate."

When they were in grade school, Myrtie wouldn't let Kate inside her house because she was Catholic.

"The baby weighed six pounds three ounces and they named her Rose," Sarah said. She wanted her grandmother to say it again.

"I hope she's raised in a Christian home," said Myrtie.

"Catholics are Christians, Grandmother," Sarah said.

"I just wish everybody could have been here today," Myrtie said. Her husband had been dead nineteen years.

"I'm giving my boy that Remington of mine," Lloyd said to Veachel.

"I expect he'll need it, living up there in the woods," Vera said. She shivered. Peter was living somewhere near Ottawa in a cabin with some girl. They had only a wood stove for heat. For health reasons, he ate a whole clove of garlic every day.

"That's mighty generous of you," said Veachel. "I've had my eye on that gun for some time."

"I started Peter out young like Dad did us," said Lloyd. The story went that when Veachel was given a new BB gun, Lloyd got his old one.

"You have to," Veachel said, "if you expect them to have any respect for firearms later on."

"He can handle a gun all right," said Lloyd.

At the age of seven Peter shot a possum and Lloyd said they had to eat it. Nobody believed him until Irene put it in a pot and boiled it with sweet potatoes for dinner.

"I used to get a kick out of it," Veachel said, "but I don't hunt anymore."

Then Vera asked, as if she were somehow the victim, when anybody thought Peter would come home. "Remember the time he locked himself inside the old icebox on Mother's back porch?" she said. If the icebox had been out behind the shed where Ansel wanted to put it, the grown-ups speculated, or if they'd not been paying attention, they wouldn't have gotten to Peter on time.

"The Lord watches over them. I'm so thankful for that. He watches over us all," Myrtie said. A leather Bible lay next to her plate. She touched it. Then she looked at something not in the room.

"You're right about that, Mother," said Veachel.

"If He hadn't been with me all these years, I don't know what I would have done," Myrtie said.

The bright day and the hard look of concrete rolled toward them fast. Myrtie had forgotten to set the hand brake when she and Ansel got out to dump trash into the ravine. They left Sarah and Laura in the backseat. There was no noise, only the taste of metal. Sarah watched her grandmother chase them, waving her arms in silence. Myrtie fell on the highway and got up with her shins bleeding. Their grandfather couldn't run. He had jaundice at the time, though jaundice wasn't what killed him. Cigarettes killed him. Sarah and Laura were only four. They weren't hurt when the car swerved into the trees.

They stood in the road until Lloyd got there. It was the first time Sarah had felt the highway under her feet. She felt displaced. They weren't supposed to stand in the road, but their father didn't say anything. He was so upset he couldn't talk. He never had been able to get angry with his mother. A week later their grandfather went into the hospital and never came out.

"One of these days this old world is going to end and He's coming back to take us home to glory," Myrtie said. "It tells us in the Bible, 'For ye are dead, and your life is hid with Christ in God. When Christ, who is our life, shall appear, then shall ye also appear with him in glory.'"

"Amen, Mother," said Veachel.

"We had a lot of fun fishing," Myrtie said.

"Dad really loved to fish, didn't he?" Veachel said.

"He surely did. I still have his canvas fishing stool."

"Who wants chocolate cake," Irene asked standing up. She looked especially elegant in the surroundings.

"We all do," said Vera.

"I don't," Sarah said.

"None for me," said Marianne.

"His favorite place was under that old beech up toward the dam," said Veachel.

"I remember that," Lloyd said. He folded his napkin into a neat package and laid it by his plate.

"Aunt Mildred and Aunt Margaret used to go along. They didn't fish. They just watched the river," said Veachel.

Sarah saw them in identical sun dresses and hats, a woman appearing twice in the August sun on a muddy river bank. She stood holding herself as if she were cold.

"Had he gone with A&P yet or was he still over at the

shoe factory?" Vera asked. She was scraping plates and stacking them on the table in front of her.

"He managed the A&P until after the Depression," said Lloyd.

"That was about the time Uncle Oscar went to Brazil," Veachel said. Oscar was Myrtie's older brother.

"We spent a lot of happy hours fishing. Nobody fishes anymore," Myrtie said.

"Why they do, Mother," said Vera. "You just don't fish anymore."

"Why don't I fish anymore?" Myrtie asked.

"How's your love life?" Marianne asked with her hands in the dishwater. Sarah was drying.

"Not bad." They had gone to Girl Scout camp together and started their periods a few weeks apart. Who did Marianne like best? "How's yours?" Sarah asked.

"Super," said Marianne. She used to talk a lot but after she got married she stopped, as if sex had something to do with it.

"How was your trip to Arizona?" Sarah asked. The kitchen felt empty.

"Fantastic," Marianne said.

She was the best play doctor. She performed intricate operations with her small soft fingers, touching here and there with concentration. Under Marianne's fingers, Sarah stopped breathing. She still remembered the exquisite sensation of wishing to be Marianne's only patient.

Sarah hung the dishtowel over a chair and went to the bathroom. She shut the door and sat on the edge of the tub.

"Did they have to fly over Cuba?" Vera asked in the dining room. Her voice didn't sound that far away.

"Cuba is further south," Irene said.

"Then they didn't fly over Cuba like we thought," said Vera.

A chair scraped across the floor. Sarah wasn't going to come to Myrtie's for dinner, then at the last minute she came.

"Her postcard said they'd been snorkeling," Lloyd said.

"What's snorkeling?" Myrtie asked in an offended voice.

Sarah stood. She opened her grandmother's medicine cabinet. It contained toothpaste, Noxzema, gauze, iodine, and milk of magnesia.

"She said the coral reefs are just full of toxic fish," said Irene. "Several people have come down with food poisoning."

"Coral is beautiful, Mother," said Lloyd. "It grows like a plant under water. When they bring it up it's hard as rock."

"That's because it's dead," said Veachel.

"Beauty is where you find it," said Myrtie. "I like my house."

"There's a lot of beauty right around here, especially this time of year," Veachel said.

Sarah sat back down on the edge of the tub, her chin in her hands. The smell of Myrtie's orange blossom dusting powder made her sullen. She watched the door with the feeling that someone was going to walk in on her.

"Did you hear the governor vetoed the bill to legalize church bingo?" Vera asked sounding distant.

"Does that mean we're going to have it or not going to have it?" Myrtie said.

"Not going to have it," Vera said, her voice close again.

"Bingo is gambling," said Myrtie.

"No it isn't Mother," said Vera.

Sarah stood and looked at herself in the mirror. She had the small Broderhouse eyes, but not the slant. Marianne had the slant and Myrtie's heart-shaped face. They all had Myrtie's nose. Sarah opened her eyes wide and stretched her mouth into a silent scream. Her face was all mouth and teeth and tongue. Unexpectedly, she did not look horrible but she thought she saw death. The loneliness in it was worse than anything.

"Grain shipments have been quarantined because of the cereal leaf beetle infestation," Irene said beyond the door. "That's going to hurt a lot of farmers."

Seven

"If we didn't have you, Lloyd," Margaret said with emotion, "we would have to pay an exterminator."

Sarah aimed the flashlight at her father's hands. She wanted to be necessary to him.

"I'm glad to do it," Lloyd said under the sink.

"I heard it go off in the middle of the night and I couldn't get back to sleep thinking what must be down here," said Margaret.

"You got him all right," said Lloyd.

"Do you think he's the only one?" Sarah asked watching her father.

"I hate to say it but where there's one there's usually three or four," Lloyd said. He came out with a dead mouse in the trap.

"That's what I thought," said Sarah.

"Are you going to throw it away trap and all?" Margaret asked.

"It's a disposable trap but I'll reset it if you want me to," Lloyd said.

"A penny saved is a penny earned," said Margaret.

"She was afraid to come down this morning," Mildred said. "I had to clear the way."

"You'd have thought there was a brass band in the kitchen the way she carried on," said Margaret. "It reminded me of Myrtie."

Myrtie yelled from the top of the basement stairs to frighten the mice out of sight. She said one of them could jump out at her. The grandchildren were not allowed to play in her basement after the day she found a dead bat in the clothespin bag.

"Get rid of it Lloyd," Margaret said.

"I'm going to," said Lloyd.

"While you're here," said Mildred, "could you take a look at the washing machine? It quits before spin and the clothes come out heavy."

Myrtie had also scared them to death about getting their fingers caught in the ringer. It was electric and she was afraid she would forget how to stop it in an emergency. She told them their fingers would come out flat.

"What's that noise?" Margaret said.

"I heard it too," said Sarah.

"If one ran over my foot I would die," said Mildred.

"There it went," Margaret whispered. "It ran from the refrigerator to the stove." She stood on the old church pew they used as a bench at the kitchen table.

Sarah climbed on the bench too. "Do something Dad," she said.

"Okay everybody," Lloyd said. "Don't panic."

"A hamster crawled up into my bedsprings when I had the mumps and chewed a hole in my sheet," Sarah said. "I heard it gnawing but nobody would believe me."

Lloyd had made a ping-pong table from a sheet of plywood and set it up on sawhorses out in the garage. Peter and Laura were looking for a ping-pong ball the day they smelled the baby hamsters decomposing in Lloyd's army surplus canteen.

"This canteen's ruined," Lloyd said before leaving for work. By then he was a private pilot.

"Forgive me," Sarah prayed an even number of times in the closet. She had wished the hamsters would die. For a long time guilt seemed connected to the ping-pong table.

"They climb curtains too," Mildred said.

"I will not stay in this house another night," said Margaret.

"What do you think they're going to do?" Lloyd said. He pulled out the stove and looked behind it.

"They carry the bubonic plague," she said.

"It's actually fleas that carry the plague," Lloyd said. "Not many people realize that."

"It doesn't matter if you ask me," Margaret said.

"I couldn't stand it if one of them bit me on the ankle," said Mildred. She covered her heart.

"Let's not get carried away," Lloyd said. He shoved the stove back.

"I don't think we are," said Margaret. "To me the problem is real."

"I didn't say the problem wasn't real Aunt Margaret," he said. "What I'm saying is that we've caught one and seen one. That makes only two."

"You said yourself there are probably more," said Margaret.

"I know I said that." Lloyd pulled a red bandanna out of his back pocket and wiped his face.

"I don't know which is worse," said Margaret. "Worrying about them during the day or at night."

"Worrying about them at night is worse," said Sarah.

"I want all of you to go into the parlor," Lloyd said. He folded his handkerchief and put it back in his pocket.

"What's he doing in there?" Margaret asked in the parlor.

"It sounds like he's opening paper sacks the way they do in the grocery store," said Mildred.

"I don't hear anything now," said Margaret.

Outside a car went by. A moment later it honked and up the street someone shouted.

"That would be Jim on his way home for lunch," Mildred said.

"Is it noon already?" Margaret asked. "I didn't hear the shoe factory whistle go off."

Sarah listened for sounds of her father in the kitchen. He always came right over when his aunts called, as if he couldn't do enough for them. As if they had never forgiven him for something.

Eight

They walked through his yard toward the farmhouse. Beside the garage was a pile of scrap metal. Sarah had known Kevin Porter since grade school. He was the kid whose mouth was always wet. They touched shoulders and moved apart.

"I don't want a story about me in that fascist rag," Kevin said. He rolled up the sleeves of his blue work shirt.

"You're an artist," she said. "People want to know about you."

"No they don't," he said.

They went in the back door into his kitchen. Broken leaves and twigs lay around the wood stove. Sarah watched the light come through the window over the sink. She wanted to be the woman who lived there and canned fruit into mason jars.

Kevin put crushed eggshells into the coffee grounds. "Why are you doing that?" she asked.

"It's something my mother taught me," he said. He tied the grounds up in a piece of cheesecloth and put the bundle into the coffeepot. "I do it for love. Love is the easiest thing in the world. There's so much of it. The world is love."

She didn't believe him but she smiled. She watched him put more wood into the stove. He did it gently. When the coffee was ready, he filled two chipped cups. She took a sip of coffee.

"This is delicious," she said. She inhaled the steam.

They carried the cups into the living room. The room was empty except for a large metal sculpture in the middle. Sarah looked at the tangle of pipe. She studied the light in the room. "Could I photograph this piece?" she asked. She set the coffee cup on the floor.

"I call it *Sisters*," Kevin said. "I wonder if they know each other's thoughts."

"Sometimes they do," she said. She was on her knees. Kevin squatted beside her. She shot several frames.

"I want to be that close to someone," he said.

"It looks dangerous to me," she said.

"I got the idea from an article about some Siamese twins out in L.A. They're attached at the skull."

Sarah moved around the sculpture taking more pictures.

"I want a woman in this house," said Kevin. "I want children. Imagine how satisfying it would be. You would never be lonely."

"Yes you would," she said. She looked at him. In the third grade he kissed her behind the piano but he was someone to be avoided.

She put the lens cap back on her camera. She always put the lens cap back on her camera. She set the camera by the coffee cup. When she saw how the china cup and the camera looked together on the wood floor, she wanted to take a picture.

"Sit down," Kevin said. He took off his glasses.

She sat on the floor. He untied her shoe and took it off. He pulled her sock off slowly. It seemed to come endlessly from under her jeans. It was a knee sock.

"You have a beautiful foot," he said.

He moved his hand under her jeans toward her knee. She saw her legs around his back holding him, his fingers wrapped with her hair, their white bodies on the floor before the sculpture.

He kissed her ear. "Your ear is so small. A child's ear," he said. She watched his face move toward hers. Without glasses his eyes were small and naked like an old man's.

"Kiss my eyes," she said.

He kissed her eyes. Tears stung them and she had the feeling of a dream again. She was on a daybed with a stranger trying to make love. Their arms and legs hung off the bed and they could never find the right position. She knew she would never get off the daybed.

Nine

"I'm going to get a white sofa and put it where you're standing," Laura said.

Sarah was standing in the middle of the living room. She had on a blue satin blouse.

"Or maybe it would go better in front of the windows. What do you think?" Laura wore a burgundy pullover with a starched pink collar showing. The outfit was tasteful but too neat. Was she under a strain?

"Either place," said Sarah.

In one corner sat a leather armchair, a smoking stand, and a floor lamp. Across the room was a baby grand and a rubber plant. Outside the day was bright.

"Matthew doesn't want a white sofa," said Laura. "He wants brown and rust. Men always want brown and rust.

Choosing furniture is our biggest problem." She leaned against the door jamb.

"I can imagine," Sarah said. Laura was framed by the doorway but she was off center.

"Matthew smokes his pipe and drinks cognac in his chair after dinner," Laura said.

"How scenic."

"And I play the *Moonlight* Sonata. I only play the first part because then it gets too hard. But he doesn't know the difference."

"What if you played 'Old Devil Moon'?" Sarah asked. She smiled.

"He doesn't want to hear anything but the *Moonlight* Sonata."

"At least our piano lessons came in handy," Sarah said. It seemed they played *Polonaise* as a duet for years.

"We're going to paper the bedroom in navy blue and burlap," Laura said. She left the doorway.

"That sounds yummy," Sarah called after her. "Yummy" was a word their mother used.

In the kitchen Laura pulled the casserole out of the oven, looked at it, and shoved it back in. Sarah stared at the braided garlic in the window. She would give anything not to have worn the satin blouse. It would look better on a juggler.

Laura was slicing a cucumber. "You can come here anytime," she said in her dreamy voice. "Our house is your house." She smiled at the cucumber.

Sarah lived in two rooms of her own over a barbershop. She looked at the window. A spider was spinning itself down past the glass, its thread invisible in the light. She felt vague. The only way to be free was to get angry.

"Did I tell you Stanley's coming for a visit?" Laura's voice sounded far away.

"Oh Stanley," Sarah said. Why had she gotten into bed with him in the first place? She took a deep breath.

"He's bringing some woman and they're staying a week," said Laura.

"Tell them that's too long."

"Matthew told me to read *Time* so I would have something interesting to talk about when they get here."

"Doesn't that make you angry?" Sarah asked. Vinnie Goldman had told her the same thing the day he found out she didn't have any political opinions except Lloyd's. Vinnie said she ought to take more of an interest in life.

"Matthew's right," said Laura. "When the conversation turns to politics, I can't follow." She pulled an aluminum pan out from under the sink.

"Can he make beef jerky?" Sarah asked. "Does he know how to backpaddle a canoe?"

"Matthew can't swim," said Laura.

"Bring up synchronized swimming. Start a discussion on silent canoeing," said Sarah.

Laura sighed and greased the pan. "Did I tell you Matthew's mother brought him a month's supply of homemade frozen dinners? They drove down in their Winnebago and lived in our driveway for a week. They drank all our gin. We had to park in the street."

Sarah was sitting on the stool by the stove. The buzzer went off.

"They taped a commentary of their trip and played it back for us." Laura opened the refrigerator door and stood in front of it. "Things like, just passed the Texaco station at the Bridgeport exit. And things in Spanish. Evelyn's a Spanish teacher. She speaks Spanish to Harold and the boys but they've never tried to understand her." Laura found the salad oil and turned around. She was backlit and surrounded by food.

"What's wrong?" Sarah asked.

"Why do we always pick men who want to improve us?" she said with tears in her eyes.

"You're a newlywed," Sarah said. "I've heard the first few months are very emotional."

"This is supposed to be the happiest time of my life," Laura said.

Sarah got up and put her arm around her sister. "Things will probably get better," she said.

"I wasn't complaining."

"You can complain to me anytime," Sarah said.

"No. I'm not going to be one of those bitter wives." She looked at Sarah's blouse. "Would you like to borrow one of my sweaters?" she asked. "Bruce is coming."

"What's wrong with my blouse?"

"Your hair looks nice though," said Laura. "Who cut it? I need to get mine cut."

Sarah sat back down by the stove. Being twins seemed to be something they would never outgrow.

"Why don't you find your own hairdresser," she said.

"What?"

"I said find your own hairdresser."

"You're kidding," Laura said. She looked at the refrigerator. She looked at the stove. "You can't imagine how that makes me feel."

"I'm sorry," Sarah said.

"What made you say that?"

One day when they were in college, she found Laura going through her jewelry box without asking. She had wanted to scream but she asked instead, "Do you want to borrow my pearls?" It didn't seem right to feel so angry.

"Sometimes I feel crowded," she said. "I just want some privacy."

"I'm not crowding you," Laura said. She opened a drawer and looked inside. "Your feelings are wrong."

Sarah couldn't move, she felt so full of bees. She felt invisible.

"In fact I think your feelings are immature and petty," said Laura.

"This isn't as bad as it sounds," Sarah said. But she was afraid that it was.

The toilet in the back of the house flushed and Matthew walked into the kitchen with the *Wall Street Journal* under one arm. Lloyd always carried *Field & Stream*.

"What's wrong?" he said looking at Laura. "What's wrong?" he asked Sarah.

"She's in a bad mood," said Laura.

"No I'm not," said Sarah.

"You could cut the air in here with a knife," Matthew said.

"She wants the name of my hairdresser," Sarah said to him.

"Why don't you give it to her?" he asked.

Sarah shrugged. "I think she ought to find her own."

"Sarah's feeling insecure," Matthew said.

"I don't even want to know the name of her hairdresser now," Laura said.

"My dad gave me some advice once," said Matthew. He pulled out a chair and sat down at the kitchen table. He put his feet on the table. He had on his cowboy boots. "He said son, break the mirror."

"What is that supposed to mean?" Laura asked.

Sarah looked at Matthew's hair, his ear, the smooth line of his jaw. "Is this mirror inside you or outside you?" she asked.

"Who knows," Laura said with irritation.

"We have a tendency to see ourselves as we think other people see us," said Matthew.

"Is that it," Sarah said.

"If you broke the mirror, you'd be like the crazy person who lives in the woods and wears long underwear in the summer," said Laura.

Matthew looked at Sarah as if they had something in common. For a minute she was glad and then she wasn't. If he didn't think Laura was bright, why had he married her?

"You think I'm stupid, don't you?" Laura said to him.

"She thinks I think she's stupid, therefore she feels stupid," Matthew said.

Sarah imagined his hair on fire. "If you don't mind," she said to Laura, "I would like to borrow one of your sweaters after all."

Her blouse wasn't ordinary and for an instant she wanted

to put it back on, but Laura needed her. So she folded it into a small package and stuffed it in her purse. She pulled on Laura's sweater and went back out to the kitchen. Laura was tearing up lettuce for the salad. The television was on loud in the other room.

"I try to make him happy," Laura said. "Why isn't he happy?"

Sarah put her arm around her sister. "I got my hair cut at the Fashion Salon. Ask for Judy," she said in Laura's sweater with her arm around Laura.

Ten

Harriet Sawyer never stopped typing on her manual. She looked at Sarah and then she looked at Jack. Another woman would have looked at Jack first. He was wearing a black motorcycle jacket and blue jeans. He had curly black hair. He had slender wrists and ankles. He could have been a dancer or a boxer. He could have been a hundred things.

He sat on Sarah's desk and touched her cheek with one finger. She drew back. It was ten o'clock in the morning.

"Please go," she said thinking of his wife in the doorway.

Esther Beeber looked alert in classified ads. She went to the First Christian Church with Lloyd and Irene. Jack grinned at Esther.

"Meet me after work," he said to Sarah.

"I can't," she said.

He stood. She thought he was going to shout at her.

"I could meet you at Marvin's Bar," she said. "Five o'clock."

"I don't suppose I'll have much trouble finding it in this town," he said.

"I don't suppose you will," she said.

"How are you today?" he said to Esther Beeber as he walked out.

Sarah watched him through the large front window beyond the words *Daily Courier* painted on the glass. At the curb he spit on the sidewalk like her father did and crossed the street looking purposeful. Jack had no purpose, she thought. He kicked the mud off his boots on the opposite curb and walked out of view.

"It's seductive for a man not to seduce a woman," Harriet said. She took a bite from her club sandwich.

"Is that what it is," Sarah said. They were sitting in a booth in the sandwich shop next to the *Courier* building. She put catsup on her grilled cheese. She ate grilled cheese with catsup when she was upset.

Harriet lit a cigarette. She blew out some smoke and watched it. She took a sip of coffee and tapped ashes onto the rest of her sandwich.

"I had the feeling I was making a mistake," Sarah said. "But I did it anyway."

"Maybe it was a mistake you needed to make," said Harriet.

Jack had sat on her couch in the beige room at the lake

and watched television every night for a week. He didn't ask for anything, not even a glass of water. He was a man on her couch. Finally Sarah asked him if he wanted to make love to her.

Harriet took a long drag. "Or maybe it wasn't even a mistake," she said.

Sarah watched the clock above the grill. It had to be a mistake because their lovemaking was strange.

"My mother said it was a mistake for me to live up at the lake. I stayed in a rooming house and worked as a waitress," she said.

"Are you in danger?" Harriet asked.

For a moment Sarah felt that maybe she was. "If I had listened to my mother this never would have happened," she said.

"It would have happened someday," said Harriet.

Sarah sighed. "I like you Harriet," she said.

"You like me because I don't bullshit you," said Harriet. She got up and put her raincoat over her shoulders. "Why do you like this man?"

"He told me I was special. He said I'm the woman he was looking for."

Harriet stubbed her cigarette out in the ashtray.

"He's so sure of himself, he tells me who I am," Sarah said.

"And who is that?"

"Someone who shouldn't spend her life in this town."

"Isn't that something you already knew?" Harriet got out another cigarette and lit it. She waved the match out.

"You ought to quit smoking, Harriet."

She walked past the silent amplifiers and drums. She smelled the smell of sour apples. But it wasn't apples. It was spilled beer.

"How you doing?" Marvin said. He was putting beer in glass bottles into the cooler.

"Fine," she said. She thought about turning around and walking out but she didn't. She walked toward Jack. He was playing pool alone at the back of the bar. He knocked a ball into a side pocket and then he looked up and saw her.

Sarah unbuttoned her coat. "Why did you come?" she asked.

Jack took aim again. "I want you to go away with me," he said.

She laughed. "You can't just walk into my life and ask me to go with you after what happened at the lake," she said. She put her hands in her coat pockets.

"I didn't know my wife was coming to the lake," he said. "You can't blame that on me." He sent the red ball to the opposite end of the table.

"I'm not the kind of person who would walk out on a job," she said.

"Yes you are," he said. "You just don't know it."

"You don't know me as well as you think you do," she said.

He grinned. "Don't you recognize Jack Summers?"

"Who is Jack Summers?" she said.

"He is your destiny." He bent over the table again. Sarah watched his hands. She needed a destiny. Jack knocked in the last ball and laid the cue on the table. "Come over to the motel with me," he said.

"I can't go to the motel with you," she said. "This is my hometown."

"Then don't come," he said.

Sarah didn't look at Marvin as they walked out, but she was sure he was watching them.

"He knows my dad," she said outside. She looked at the sky. She looked at the woods.

"Lucky guy," said Jack. He got on his bike and started it. He put on his helmet. She remembered riding the highway by the lake. They wore cotton tee-shirts and the wind was warm on their skin.

She knew she shouldn't but she followed him to the Twilight Motor Court. She watched a man come out of the office but she didn't know him. She was glad Jack's room was in the back. She parked next to his bike and went in. The room was cold and beige like the rooms at the lake. He turned on the television with the sound off and unpacked his knapsack. She sat on the bed.

"I'm going to Canada," he said.

She had never been to Canada. Jack went into the bathroom. She heard water running. He came out with a glass of water and took a pill.

"My brother lives in Canada," she said. "He's a conscientious objector."

"You mean he's a draft dodger."

She looked at the window. The curtains were closed. They were gold. She watched the silent weatherman on television. "If you're sick you shouldn't be riding around up there in the cold," she said.

He laughed. "Why do women always want to take care of me?"

"I don't want to take care of you," she said.

"Yes you do," he said. He took some underwear out of his pack and refolded it. "Can you do some laundry for me?"

She looked at the shabby furniture. She looked at the lamp. She listened to the room, the sound of the zipper on his pack being zipped.

"I guess I can," she said.

Then she heard a car pull up outside and sit idling. She went to the window and looked out at the edge of the curtain.

"Christ," she said. "Oh Jesus."

"What," said Jack.

"It's my father," she said. She held herself. "Damn. That bartender told him."

"So what does your old man have to do with this?" Jack said.

"You don't understand," Sarah said. Her father was in the vicinity. She felt his influence.

"Your life isn't his business," Jack said. He kicked off his boots. He unbuckled his belt.

She listened to the sound of her father driving away.

Eleven

The music was too loud. Sarah watched some dancers slide through the light from the jukebox. She and Jack had never danced. Dancing didn't seem right for them. She looked toward the door for Jack and saw Matthew making his way through the crowd by the bar.

"Miles of flat country with telephone poles is a satisfying image," the drunk woman next to her said. "This stool is taken," the woman told Matthew.

"I'll leave when your friend comes," Matthew said. He took off his ski parka.

"It isn't for my friend," said the woman. She had straight black hair. "It's for hers."

"What's so funny," Sarah said.

"I find this humorous," Matthew said.

"I didn't think he had a sense of humor," the woman said in an accusing voice.

Matthew took Sarah's arm. "Come on. Let's dance."

"I don't feel like dancing," she said. She felt his fingers tighten around her arm.

"Yes you do," he said.

They walked onto the dance floor. The floor was slick with sawdust. Other dancers pressed them together. Matthew's arm was hard against her back and his body was hard against hers. She wondered how she felt to him. He kept his arm around her when the song ended and they danced the next dance. In the dim light she watched his face move toward hers. Was he pretending she was Laura? She opened her mouth slightly.

"Why don't you let me get you out of here?" he whispered.

"I'm waiting for Jack," she said.

"You're making a mistake," he said. "Isn't this guy married?"

"Laura wasn't supposed to tell anyone that," she said.

Matthew pulled her closer. She hid her face against his chest. With Laura telling her secrets, her life didn't belong to her anymore. Matthew held her in both arms now, his mouth on her neck.

"You're too good for him," he whispered.

"You don't know anything about him," she said.

She saw Jack unbuckle his belt and unzip his pants. He looked as if he might hurt her. All at once she didn't want to stay in a noisy bar with strangers.

"Go out and get in my truck. I'll be right there," Matthew said.

"I can't stand him up," she said.

"Yes you can," he said. He took hold of her shoulders and pushed her toward the door.

Sarah walked through the crowd. The front door opened and a tall man came in. It was Roy Thomas in his cowboy hat. He held the door for her and watched her walk under his arm.

"How are you this evening?" he asked.

"Fine," she said.

"You aren't leaving already, are you?" he said.

"I think so," she said.

The seats in Matthew's truck were stiff with cold and made noise as she got in. The truck was full of noise and she felt as if she had spent most of her life there, doing first what one person told her and then the next.

"I think you're doing the right thing," Matthew said when he got there. He started the engine and pulled out of the parking lot. He turned onto the highway. It was beginning to rain. Sarah watched the rain in the headlights. Matthew continued in his nasal tone, giving her advice.

He turned out the lights in front of her apartment above the barbershop. He sat with one arm over the steering wheel, the other on the back of the seat. He touched her shoulder. "I wonder what would have happened if I had met you first," he said.

"I never thought about it," Sarah said.

"Sure you have," he said. He nudged her shoulder. She looked at the reflection of her face in the windshield. She could see it in the light from the radio.

"Come on," said Matthew. "What did you think?"

"I wondered if you would have chosen me," she said.

"Did you want me to?"

"No," she said. "I just wondered if you would have." She opened the door. The interior light came on. Matthew grimaced.

"Wait a minute," he said.

She got out of the truck and shut the door. She walked toward the steps going up to her apartment. She wanted Matthew to watch her walk away from him.

"Don't you think it's using bad judgment to meet your friends at a motel?" Irene said.

Sarah stopped drinking her coffee. They were sitting in her mother's kitchen. Sarah looked at her mother. Yes she thought it was bad judgment but she had done it anyway. It was also bad judgment to sit in a parked truck with her sister's husband.

"Your father told me he saw your car at the Twilight Motor Court last week," said Irene. "Was it your car?"

"Is he following me around or what?" Sarah asked.

"He wanted to make sure you weren't in any danger."

"I was at the Twilight visiting a friend," said Sarah.

"Couldn't you visit your friend someplace else? Couldn't you meet at a restaurant?" Irene asked.

"Mother. Why was Dad following me?"

"Someone called and said you were being harassed by a motorcyclist."

"He's someone I met at the lake last summer."

"Then why don't you bring him by so we can meet him?"

"It's complicated."

Irene sighed. "We aren't secretive people. If you can't bring him by, there must be something wrong."

"If you met him, you wouldn't like him."

"Then why do you like him?"

Sarah hugged herself. "Because he's different."

"Why do you put me in this position, Sarah? Sometimes I think you do it on purpose."

Sarah was angry but her mother didn't like anger. "I don't think I do it on purpose," she said in a small voice.

"Why can't you be satisfied to live like everybody else?"

"Life would be too disappointing." Sarah got up and poured herself more coffee from the percolator.

"Everyday life is all there is. When are you going to learn that?" Irene said. "I think you'll find that feelings don't have to be dramatic to be satisfying."

"Tell Dad he doesn't need to follow me around anymore."

"Your dad doesn't follow you around." Irene stood.

Sarah listened to her mother's footsteps on the wooden stairs to the basement. Her mother was a good and reasonable person. She always did the right thing. Sarah wanted to do the right thing, but doing the right thing bored her.

Twelve

"*Esoteric* is intended for or understood by a chosen few," Matthew read. "It applies to ideas, doctrines, or literature and cannot be applied to people as you used it, Laura. Kate might be enigmatic but not esoteric." He closed the dictionary beside his plate and looked at Sarah.

"I'd say Kate is elusive," Sarah said. She thought of his mouth on her neck. She should have eluded him. She shouldn't have let him hold her the way he did.

"Immature?" Bruce asked.

"More noodles?" said Laura.

"This stroganoff is delicious," said Bruce.

"I'm curious to know what you meant," Matthew said to Laura. He leaned back in his chair like a businessman.

"If I could have thought of a better word, Matthew, I would have used it," Laura said. She passed the noodles.

"Ephemeral," Sarah said, feeling ashamed. When a man took an interest in her, she lost her will. She was going to have to stop it.

"I think that's what she meant," said Bruce.

"I don't think ephemeral can be applied to people either," said Matthew.

"Erotic?" said Bruce.

"Eroticism is disgusting," Laura said and took a careful bite.

"Erratic?" said Bruce.

"Effervescent," Sarah said. "Effervescent can be applied to humans."

"Effervescent people are out of control," Laura said.

"Eccentric," Bruce said.

"Kate is anything but eccentric," said Laura. "All she ever wanted to do was get married and have babies." She put down her fork.

"That's because her father died when she was young," Sarah said.

"Elfin," said Matthew. "Kate is elfin." He folded his hands under his chin and leaned forward. Everybody stared at him. It was his birthday.

Laura only pretended to play, bending over the keyboard with a grimace then leaning back and closing one eye. For the skit they had dressed in black. Sarah took a James Jones novel from Matthew's bookcase. She stood by the piano and pretended to read aloud. Matthew sat in his leather armchair smoking a pipe and Bruce sat on the floor beside him. The room was silent.

"Is this it?" Matthew said.

Sarah raised her hand and Laura began to play. Sarah read a few lines aloud then dropped her hand and began to mouth the words. At the same time Laura dabbed her fingers over the keys without playing. Sarah raised her hand and dropped it, raised it and dropped it. There was sound then silence. They did it again and again.

"This is boring," said Matthew. He stood up. "You can't just repeat the same thing over and over."

"Sit down, Matthew," Laura said. "I can't play with you standing up."

In Sarah's dream the audience sat on the floor in semicircles in the dark. Outside in the lobby, beer and soft pretzels were being sold. Two white grand pianos sat on stage with their keyboards a few feet apart. Laura wore red and Sarah wore black. They had on their berets. Together they walked onto the curved stage and sat down, backs touching.

Sarah played a run in the treble. She always played treble and Laura played bass. They performed as fast as they could with four hands. When one grew tired the other played harder. It was their best duet. They finished playing and turned with shrewd smiles to the audience. But the audience had vanished.

"Some people might think there should be more to it," Bruce said, "but I liked it the way it was."

"Let's have some champagne," Laura said taking a bow.

"I don't want any champagne," said Matthew.

"But it's your birthday," she said.

"I know it's my birthday," he said.

Sarah sat next to Bruce on the carpet and waited. They heard Laura and Matthew arguing in the kitchen. Laura called him a baby. He told her to get off his back.

"He's pretty rough on her sometimes," Bruce said.

Sarah shrugged. For a moment she didn't feel sorry for her sister and then she did.

"Why does he do it?" she asked.

"He's used to getting his way," said Bruce. "He was Mom's favorite." He shrugged. He seemed to be watching the piano legs.

Sarah touched his shoulder.

"Did you know I wanted to marry you?" Bruce asked. He looked at her with his big earnest face.

"You loved Laura," she said.

"It sounds terrible, I know, wanting to marry you when I couldn't have Laura."

"I've imagined myself married to you," Sarah said. "I imagine myself married to everyone."

"Do you ever look at Laura and think you're seeing yourself?" Bruce asked.

"She's always careful about how much her lips move when she talks. I thought that was stupid. Then I saw myself in a home movie doing the same thing. We have never looked so much alike."

"It must be a strain having someone around who looks just like you. People confuse Matthew and me and we don't even look alike," said Bruce.

Once when Sarah was in St. Louis, a stranger stopped her on the street and hugged her. They both had on heavy coats. She watched his breath on the cold air. He said he had always wanted to go to bed with her, but now he was married. They laughed it off. As it turned out, he and Laura had worked together one summer in a VA hospital. Sarah never told him she wasn't Laura.

"When we were kids, we shared everything," she said. "All our possessions were identical. I always felt in danger of not being loved."

"I can see a big difference between you two," Bruce said.

"What is it?" she asked.

Bruce covered one eye. "She has more fun."

Sarah shrugged.

"Did you have a crush on Matthew?" Bruce asked. "It's okay if you did."

"I only felt left out," she said.

Bruce took her hand, rubbed the back of it with his thumb. "I think we ought to go somewhere," he said. "Just the two of us. I wouldn't be pretending you were Laura, if that's what you think."

"Champagne everybody," Matthew said, coming back with a green bottle held over his head.

The lights went out. Into the room came a cake, aflame. Laura's face above the candles was hopeful. The candles flickered as she sang, her voice sweet and afraid. Then the cork popped into the dark and hit the ceiling.

Everybody said "Ah."

"What is that smell?" Sarah asked in the dark apartment. Bruce turned on a light. From another room came the sound of a guitar being played one string at a time.

"I don't smell anything," he said.

Dishes were stacked on the counter and in the sink. A newspaper lay open on the kitchen table. The kitchen and the living room were one room. All the chairs and the sofa faced the television. Everything was the same color.

"Can I get you something?" Bruce asked. "We have tomato juice."

"I don't like tomato juice," said Sarah. She huddled in her raincoat in the middle of the room.

"My roommate's here but he won't bother us. He's probably stoned."

"What if the police come?"

Bruce laughed. "The police aren't going to come."

"I don't understand your attitude," Sarah said. "I would be afraid living in this mess." She walked over to the sink. "Something is growing on your dishes."

"I meant to do them last weekend," said Bruce. "But time got away from me." He looked at his watch.

"Do you have an appointment?" she asked.

"I just wanted to see what time it was." He looked puzzled. "Are you nervous?"

Yes she was nervous. "I'm cold," she said.

Bruce led her to his bedroom. Still, she could hear the guitar. He unbuttoned her coat. She looked around at his stereo, his golf clubs, the humidifier. She pulled her coat close around her.

"We don't have to do it if you don't want to," Bruce said. He went over and put a record on the stereo. It was the sound of waves crashing onto a shore.

Sarah took off her coat. Bruce turned out the light. She listened to the sound of him undressing. Then she undressed. They lay close in their underwear under the blankets.

"Just hold me," she said.

"Fine," he said.

They held each other in the dark and listened to gulls cry. The ocean washed over a beach somewhere.

Thirteen

"Whoever wants this desk can have it," said Margaret. They were in the library.

Sarah wanted the desk but Laura was the one with the empty house. "Laura needs a desk," she said. She looked out the window at the sunlit day.

"She was admiring the cherry dry sink the other day," said Mildred. She stopped knitting to sort through the yarn on her lap.

"I thought it was the bird's-eye maple dresser she wanted," said Margaret. She covered her mouth with her handkerchief and coughed.

"I'd like to have the bird's-eye maple," Sarah said. Outside, a cardinal landed in the elm tree. The red color made her happy but only for a moment.

"If somebody really wants it they can have it," said Margaret.

"Where will you put your underthings?" Mildred asked.

"I'll clean out my drawers and put my underthings someplace else," said Margaret.

"There is nothing that makes me feel more organized than to clean out my underwear drawer," Mildred said.

The cardinal flew out of the elm and Sarah turned her back on the day.

"I can think of more satisfying things to do," Margaret said opening the top drawer of their old desk. She shook her head at its contents. She coughed some more. She had a bad cough.

"Every year I get in the mood to throw it all away," Mildred said. "But of course I don't. I sort out the ones with the elastic stretched. We don't buy nylon anymore. Montgomery Ward has such sturdy cotton underwear."

"Why are you going on so?" Margaret asked. "You sound like a bird."

"I'm in a talkative mood," said Mildred. "I haven't had anyone to talk to in three days."

"You two haven't spoken to each other in three days?" Sarah asked.

"Emma Cassidy is my best friend," said Mildred. She picked up her knitting again.

Margaret sighed. "When Emma's husband died, I was the one who went to her," she said.

"That was because I had the flu and couldn't go, so you went instead," said Mildred.

"You're jealous, Mildred. That's un-Christian." Margaret opened a package of cough drops and put one in her mouth.

"Emma was my best friend in school," said Mildred.

"We were all three best friends in school."

"I asked her once who she felt closer to," Mildred said knitting faster.

"I don't imagine Emma Cassidy remembers who she felt closer to. She's slipping," said Margaret.

"Your best friend is Bertha Nickelson," said Mildred.

"Bertha is a friend to me but not as close as Emma." Margaret looked at Sarah.

In college Sarah met a girl from New Jersey and they became best friends. In time, this girl became Laura's best friend too. Sarah didn't understand how this had happened and let herself be dropped. She dressed in black and wore a beret to class. She began taking pictures everywhere.

"What do you think about the piano," Margaret said. "Who wants the piano?"

"I would love to have the piano," said Sarah.

"I can't read music the way I used to but I would miss the piano," Mildred said. She pulled her sweater closer around her.

"Keep the piano for heaven's sake," Sarah said in her mother's voice.

"I'm not going to wait until I die to give my things away," said Margaret. "I want to watch people enjoy them while I'm still alive."

"If someone knows you're watching, they'll feel funny," Mildred said. She stood and put her knitting behind her in the seat of her chair. She marched out of the library.

"She doesn't play that much anymore," Margaret said.

"I think she's going to play right now," said Sarah.

"That's because you're here," Margaret said.

In the parlor Mildred started to accompany herself to

"Go Tell It on the Mountain." The sound of her voice was alarming. A siren went by in the street.

"You don't need to give your things away yet," Sarah said to Margaret. "You have a lot of good years left." She listened to the last of Mildred's song and then the silence in the house.

"Every once in a while I feel the need to play that song," Mildred said coming back into the library. She sat down and picked up her yarn. She raised her chin and started knitting again.

"Nobody is going to take your piano away from you," Sarah said.

"Sometimes I feel that they might," Mildred said. "Sometimes I feel that my things don't really belong to me."

"We don't own our things," Margaret said. "We only borrow them for as long as we are on this earth."

"That isn't what I'm talking about," said Mildred. Her lips were trembling. "Don't you ever feel that someone's in your skin with you?" she asked Sarah.

"No one can be in your skin with you," Margaret said.

"When that happens," Sarah said, "I can't make up my mind about anything. I feel panicky."

"The piano is half mine," said Mildred. "So are the desk and the bird's-eye maple dresser."

"Not the bird's-eye maple," said Margaret. "I bought it at the Simpsons' auction."

"Then the cherry dry sink is mine," said Mildred. She knitted without watching her hands. "I bought that from Evelyn Van Wyck when she moved into her apartment."

"Wasn't it Evelyn Van Wyck who gave you girls piano lessons?" Margaret asked. She pulled some papers out of the desk drawer. "For a tall woman she was fragile. Her husband was a house painter."

"The classics are one thing you can count on," Mrs. Van Wyck had told them. She touched her smile with one finger and never said anything about the composers. She wore a lavender handkerchief tucked under her watchband. In her cool parlor they behaved as if they were in church. She was always watering her house plants when they arrived Thursdays at four. Her husband moved like distant conversation through the rooms beyond the parlor, making them uneasy.

"Then one of you took lessons from that young man," Margaret said. "He played for a long time at St. Mark's and wasn't even Catholic."

"I took lessons from Mr. Williams," Sarah said. Mr. Williams was the first person she didn't have to share with Laura.

"He lived in the old rectory and put exterior awnings inside it. And a cement birdbath in the foyer," Mildred said.

"Fortunately the historical society has taken it over now," said Margaret.

"Mr. Williams was very kind to me," Sarah said. "Except once when he was in a bad mood."

Margaret closed the top desk drawer and opened a side drawer. "They say those men aren't dangerous but I think your mother did the right thing," she said.

Sarah tore down the curtains in her bedroom the day she found out Irene canceled her piano lessons with Mr. Williams. His lover was a priest.

"His lover got transferred," she said.

"Is that what they call them," Mildred said.

"Mr. Williams drove his car into the river," said Sarah. "Then he climbed out on the roof and yelled for help."

"That doesn't surprise me," Margaret said. "Someone must have saved him. He's gone to Texas." She shut the drawer.

Two years ago when Bert Sheffick was back in town, he told Irene he'd run across Gib Williams playing in a hotel bar in Houston. He'd changed his name to something Latin that meant King of Love. Bert thought this was hilarious. The King of Love was wearing a toupee, he said.

"Does anybody know the Latin for King of Love?" Sarah asked.

"Don't ask me," said Margaret.

"Jesus is the King of Love," said Mildred.

Margaret held up a pair of white kid gloves. "I'd forgotten I had these," she said. "I bought them in that shop where the five-and-dime is now."

"I believe you did buy some gloves there once," said Mildred. "But those belong to me. I bought them in Denver."

"Why I distinctly remember buying white kid gloves," Margaret said.

"What were you doing in Denver?" Sarah asked Mildred.

For a moment the only sounds in the room were the clicking of Mildred's knitting needles and the grandfather clock. The rhythms were different.

"Oh my," Margaret cried. "Where did it come from?"

A sparrow flew across the room.

"A bird in the house," Mildred whispered. "It means someone is going to die. It happened to Emma Cassidy's mother."

The sparrow flew from the top of the grandfather clock to the window and beat its wings against the glass. It kept looking up.

"It's going to break its wings," Mildred said. "It sees the sunlight and wants to be free."

"Do something," said Margaret.

"Give me your handkerchief," Sarah said to Mildred.

She took Mildred's handkerchief and walked slowly toward the bird. As she got near, it flew around the room and landed back on the clock.

"How on earth did it get in?" Margaret asked.

Sarah moved toward the grandfather clock. She raised the handkerchief but the bird flew out from under her hands and out of the library. She followed the bird back through the house to the kitchen and waited for it to settle on the windowsill over the sink. Gently she laid the embroidered handkerchief over the sparrow and cupped her hands around it. Her heart was beating fast. She felt the bird's heart beating in her hands.

Fourteen

The trees were wet and shiny against the heavy sky. Sarah sat in her car in the funeral home parking lot. She turned on the radio then she turned it off. The silence was cold. Its edge drove her out of the car. She walked slowly toward the white brick house that was the funeral home.

"Doesn't she look good?" Vera said by the casket. "They did such a nice job on her hair."

Margaret did not look good. But Veachel and Vera insisted on an open casket anyway. Lloyd said they could stand there and fan the lid for all he cared. He wasn't going to argue with them.

"She got a lot of beautiful flowers," said Irene. "Just look at all these flowers." She moved away from the coffin to read the cards.

"Margaret lived a good life," said Vera.

"What makes you say that, Aunt Vera?" Sarah asked.

"She never hurt anyone is what I mean."

"I hope I never hurt anyone either," Laura said. She put her arm around Sarah.

"I think she wasted her life," said Sarah.

"Why she didn't," said Vera. "She took care of her sister." She held her purse against her stomach.

"If someone saw her wasting her life, they should have stopped her," said Laura. She took her arm from around Sarah.

"What was her diagnosis?" the minister's wife whispered.

"Pneumonia," Laura said. "Her blood gas studies indicated severe hypoxemia and the X rays showed large areas of congestion in her lungs."

"She was as healthy as a horse before she got the flu," Sarah said.

"I don't believe it's hit Mildred yet, do you?" Vera said to the minister's wife.

Hester Blake was wearing a velveteen hat that looked like a dead leaf. Hester was once a missionary. Sarah saw herself open her mouth to be a missionary. An Italian aria came out. She couldn't stop singing in the voice that wasn't hers.

"We're just sick about it," said Hester.

"It's a blessing He took her in her sleep," Vera said.

Mildred had entered the room and was walking toward the coffin. When she got there, Vera took both her elbows like fragile, unconnected things. Mildred held her handkerchief over her mouth and searched her sister's face.

"She's with Mama and Papa in heaven," she said. "She's with Ansel and Dorothy too."

Their younger sister Dorothy had run off with a rodeo cowboy, then divorced him. After that she married a Jew and moved to Peoria to help him run a bar.

"Dorothy died in Peoria during the first war. It was March and no one could get to her," said Mildred.

"Her husband was killed in France," Vera told the minister's wife. "She died three weeks later of the Spanish flu. Neither of them ever knew the other was dead. Isn't that tragic?"

Sarah saw a cold, bare room with light from one window and outside, no one coming in the winter afternoon. "Wasn't anybody upset that she married a Jew?" she asked.

"Oh yes. They were upset," Mildred said.

Sarah and Vinnie Goldman were riding in the backseat of his older brother's compact car homecoming weekend. His brother who was fat and already bald said over one shoulder, "Nathalie and I talked it over. We decided it would be all right for you two to get married." Vinnie rolled his dark eyes and whistled to keep from laughing. His brother braked for a red light in front of the Holiday Inn. It was a beautiful fall day outside. The sister-in-law turned around with her arm across the back of the seat. She smiled and showed her perfect teeth. The light switched to green as she faced the windshield again, as Vinnie told them he and Sarah had not really made any plans. She loved and

hated Vinnie Goldman. He was her first love-hate relation-
ship. She had warned him she could never marry a Jew.

"The house feels so empty," said Mildred. "I wish they
hadn't taken her clothes."

"Who took them?" Laura asked.

"We thought it would be best to get them out of the
house right away," said Vera.

"I think it was," Hester said.

"That's what's wrong with Christianity today," said
Sarah.

"She doesn't look herself," Mildred said. She reached
into the coffin and touched Margaret's arm. "But her face is
so familiar to me. More familiar than my own. I know her
nose and mouth especially. I don't remember her eyes."

"I don't remember eyes very well either," Laura said.

"Margaret always thought her nose was too big because
it was bigger than mine," said Mildred.

"Margaret's nose wasn't too big," said Vera.

"If she felt that it was," Sarah said, "it might as well have
been."

"Margaret has been promoted," said Reverend Blake.
"Margaret has graduated." He smiled at the ceiling.

Laura uncrossed her legs next to Sarah. Then she crossed
them again. A baby cried in the back of the room.

"God said that he would satisfy. He promised satisfac-
tion. Today," Reverend Blake said. "Today, Margaret is satisfied." He clasped his hands in the air above the pulpit. He
had fat hands. "Today is the happiest day of her life. Today
is a day of great rejoicing." He opened his hands as if to
release the rejoicing.

Sarah looked at the picture of Christ on the wall behind the casket. His light brown hair was parted in the middle and looked unbearably soft. He appeared to be looking out of the picture for something, yet he wasn't looking hard. He seemed vulnerable for a man, but not extremely. Myrtie had the same oval picture in her piano room. Sarah thought she could see why so many women spent their lives devoted to Him. That no woman could have Him was irresistible but safe.

"I said, Margaret, the hood just flew off. She said, no it didn't, it only flew up. And she kept on driving." Mildred straightened the lace doily on the chair arm. "We couldn't see where we were going. I had the feeling we were swimming then we were in the car again. I thought we went over the same stretch of road twice."

"For heaven's sake," Irene said. She looked at Lloyd.

"Margaret drove with the conviction of a person on roller skates," said Mildred.

"Oh," Sarah said and felt hungry. She watched the walls rush past as she skated and skated around the vast wooden room to the horrible organ music. She felt as if she were flying. Then Laura ran into the wall and got a large splinter of wood in the palm of her hand. Wasn't Sarah going to the doctor with her sister? Kate Huckleberry wanted to know. If it was her sister, Kate said, she would go. Kate didn't have a sister. Sarah skated away. She only wanted to keep skating.

At home that night she watched Laura's hand wrapped in white gauze where it lay on the chair arm. The hand lay injured and still. A television game show was on. She should have gone with Laura. She should have gone.

"She told me she dreamed she was a helicopter pilot," Mildred said.

"Why in heaven's name would she dream that?" Vera asked.

"Why not?" Lloyd said. He was a pilot during the second war. He was standing next to Myrtie's fireplace. Everybody watched the gas flames.

"She was a speed demon at heart," said Mildred.

"She wasn't," Vera said. "I've ridden with her and so has Veachel. I thought she was a good driver."

"I'd say she was," Veachel said by the window.

"She was on her good behavior then," said Mildred.

"This is hilarious," Irene said and covered her nose.

"I broke a jar of mayonnaise on the floor one day. I had to clean it up right away, you know how oily mayonnaise is. Margaret sat in the garage and tooted at me the whole time."

"I didn't realize you two drove around by yourselves that much," said Irene.

"I'm glad I didn't know it," said Lloyd. "Gad. Can you imagine?"

"One time I looked at her behind the wheel and she was smiling like a boy we knew in primary school," said Mildred.

"Why did she stop driving?" Laura asked.

Mildred fanned herself. "Last summer we went out to that old colored man's place south of town to get canning tomatoes," she said.

"Veachel took me out there once," Vera said. "I know just the place you mean."

"We knew him when he was a boy," Mildred said. "His family lived at the top of Indian Hill. When the road got muddy, he and his daddy came out with their team of mules and pulled Papa's car up the hill."

"That's the name I was trying to remember, Veachel," said Vera. "Indian Hill."

"The day we went out, he was sitting on the porch in his rocker. When we got to him he said, see my big ears? And sat there on display."

"Does anybody understand this?" Vera asked. She looked around the room.

"Margaret looked at him like he'd just unraveled the truth. She didn't say a word. When we got home, she put the keys in the kitchen drawer and never took them out again." Mildred put her handkerchief to her mouth.

Sarah remembered seeing her great-aunts in the grocery store one day. They were picking out canned soup, two of each kind. They always picked out two of each kind. Since they rarely spoke to each other in public, people thought they could read each other's minds.

"I jumped your Plymouth off my Packard more than once," said Lloyd.

"His Packard belonged to a doctor who kept an evil sachet in the glove box," Mildred said sounding like Margaret.

"I hadn't had time to throw it out, if you recall," Lloyd said back. He crossed his arms over his chest.

"It was a pinup girl. I'd never seen one before," said Mildred.

"The carnal mind is enmity against God," Myrtie said from her chair.

"Who's going to want the Plymouth?" Veachel asked. "Do you kids want it?" He looked at Marianne.

"We really don't want the Plymouth, Daddy," she said. "I like my Toyota."

"The Plymouth would be a maintenance nightmare," said Veachel's son-in-law.

"Why it wouldn't," said Veachel. "That car's in top shape."

"Didn't one of the twins want it?" Vera asked.

"I think it would be a riot to drive around," said Laura. "I have this great hat."

"Peter is the one who needs a car," said Sarah.

"But Peter can't come back into the country to get it," said Vera.

"Maybe somebody could take it to him," said Sarah.

"Nobody can even get in touch with him," Laura said.

"Does anybody want to eat?" Irene asked. "There's gobs of food in the kitchen."

"What would you like, Aunt Mildred?" Vera said.

"I wish Mama was here to make angel food cake," Mildred said. "She made heavenly angel food."

"Food for the angels," said Myrtie. "That's a sweet thought."

"Why don't you play, Aunt Mildred," Veachel said standing up.

"Oh I don't know," she said.

"Come on," said Laura.

Mildred got up and went slowly to the piano and sat with

her hands in her lap for a moment. Then she started to play "Swing Low, Sweet Chariot." Veachel stood next to the piano and sang in his tenor voice.

"She's always played so well," Vera whispered to Irene. "Margaret just wasn't that interested."

Fifteen

"I had a dream about red fish trapped in a pool under some boulders that fell from a volcano. I'm going to find that island," Jack said over the telephone. "Are you going with me?"

Sarah opened her eyes. She was still in bed. She looked at her dresser and the pile of laundry on the chair. He sounded too close. The closeness scared her. She had told herself over and over that she wouldn't see him again.

"How will you get there? What will you live on?" she asked.

"Jesus Christ," he said. The receiver filled with sound as if he were about to hang up.

"No really. Where is this place?"

"You don't have any imagination. You don't have any dreams," he said.

"I have dreams," she said. She looked out the window at the morning beyond and saw herself kneeling in the sunlight. She was taking a picture of herself in a full-length mirror. She was in a white room in a city. Maybe she was in New York.

"We'll build a hut. I'll write poetry and at the end of each day we'll walk on the beach. We'll live on fruit and red fish."

"That may be impossible," she said.

"You really are a bitch," he said.

"Why do you treat me this way?" she asked.

He laughed. "You need it."

"I do?" she said in a hurt voice.

"I make you feel alive," he said. "I make you feel your passion and your pain."

She closed her eyes. He made her feel in danger.

"Why didn't you meet me at the bar?" he asked.

"I changed my mind."

He laughed. "You'll probably go through the rest of your life doing what other people tell you to do," he said.

"You're the one who tells me what to do," she said.

"That's because I am your destiny."

"Good-bye Jack," she said but she didn't hang up.

"I'm riding through town on Saturday. If you want to go with me, be ready," he said.

"I can't go with you," Sarah said.

"Stay then," he said. "Your destiny will go on without you."

Sarah pulled the blanket over her head and lay curled up, sniffing the dark.

"You haven't asked me where I am," Jack said in her ear.

"Where are you?"

"In the barbershop downstairs." He hung up.

When she got downstairs, Jack was getting a haircut. She watched him through the shop window. The barber bent his ear forward to trim behind it and then he clipped his neck. She had never seen his hair so short. He looked brutal and handsome. He glanced up and saw her but made no sign. She knew she was going to do what he asked.

"Let's get some coffee," he said outside.

"We can go upstairs to my place," she said. She reached up to put her arms around him but he stopped her.

"I don't want to go to your place," he said.

They walked a block to the coffee shop where college kids hung out. They sat in a high wooden booth. She looked at the words carved into the wood behind his head. She stared at his hair.

"Do I scare you?" he asked.

She looked at his hands. "Should I be afraid of you?" she asked.

"Not as long as I love you."

"Do you love me?"

He grinned. "The question is, do you love me?"

"Yes I love you," she said. Her heart was beating fast. Maybe she would feel more love after they got out of town.

"That's good," he said. He touched her arm. "I have to get out of here. I'll come back for you in two days."

"Where are you going?"

"That's none of your business."

She watched him walk away. She wanted something to happen in her life. It didn't have to be good.

"It would be a terrible mistake," said Laura.

She was sitting on the sofa before the window. The sunlight behind her was relentless. With a camera Sarah could close down the light.

"What about your job?" Laura asked.

"I can quit." Sarah got up and walked across the room. She touched a leaf on the rubber plant. "I can get another job."

"It might not be that easy," said Laura. "Be realistic."

"You don't have any respect for other people's dreams, do you," Sarah said.

"This isn't a dream," Laura said. "It's a nightmare." She pulled her knees up and hugged them.

"But I don't want to live an ordinary life."

"Nobody wants to live an ordinary life. What makes you think you're different?" Laura said.

"We're going on a motorcycle," Sarah said sitting down at the piano.

"Nobody knows anything about him."

"Dad used to ride a motorcycle," said Sarah.

"This guy is married."

"A motorcycle is perfectly good transportation. When it rains you simply put on a rain suit." She played an F-minor triad.

"I know you want me to tell you to do it," Laura said. "But I'm not going to."

"Do you remember Aunt Dorothy?" Sarah asked turning to her sister.

Laura stared at her. "You mean the Aunt Dorothy who ran off with a cowboy and a Jew?"

"Wasn't that great?" Sarah said. She looked at the ceiling. "She really lived."

"Aunt Dorothy died young," Laura said.

"What is that supposed to mean? If you really live you die young?"

"Running off might sound good now, but I imagine there was a time when Aunt Dorothy regretted it."

"I won't regret it," Sarah said.

"I imagine she hurt a lot of people."

"You think other people's feelings are more important than mine, don't you?" Sarah said. She got up and put on her jacket. She started for the door.

"It's wrong to run off with a married man. I think you're crazy," Laura shouted behind her.

"I'd rather be crazy than ordinary," Sarah said.

It was easy to leave Laura now.

II.

Sixteen

"Connie," Jack read looking at her left breast. They were in a truck stop just over the Indiana state line. Connie had a pretty face but she was overweight. She pulled two mugs out from under the counter and poured coffee into them.

"I watched you come in on your bike," she said.

"I'll just have whole wheat toast," Sarah said. An older woman was frying something on the grill. Maybe it was sausage.

"We don't have whole wheat," said Connie.

"Then I'll have white."

Jack took a sip of coffee and raised his eyebrows. "Whoa that's hot," he said and shoved the cup two inches away.

Sarah looked away. She had never seen him flirt before.

"What'll you have?" Connie asked him.

He ordered bacon and eggs.

"Two up with bacon," Connie shouted. She poured milk into a small metal pitcher. "My ex-husband and I used to tour on our bikes with this other couple," she said. "I don't know."

Jack fiddled with the ashtray. He seemed to be reading the menu written on a blackboard above the refrigerator. "You have a leather jacket, Connie?" he asked.

"An old beat up one," she said.

"You wouldn't want to sell it."

"Doesn't she have a jacket?" Connie forced the toast out of the toaster and buttered it with a brush.

Sarah looked around the restaurant. It wasn't very clean and it was drafty. The only light was from the big front window. Nobody had bothered to turn on the fluorescent lights yet. On the walls were deer antlers and a stuffed deer's rear-end.

Connie put their food in front of them.

"I'll give you twenty-five for the jacket," Jack said after a while.

"I'll let you have it for thirty bucks if you give me a ride home to get it," Connie said. "Mom," she shouted to the older woman. She didn't take her eyes off Jack. "I'll be right back."

He put his hand on the back of Sarah's neck and squeezed. Then he stood up. He and Connie walked out without talking to each other as if they were saving the truth for later.

"I'm not her mother," the woman said after they had

gone. She turned around. "Edna" was stitched on her pocket. "More coffee?"

Sarah nodded.

"Help yourself."

Sarah got up and walked around the end of the counter.

"What are you doing with him?" Edna asked. She scraped the grill. "He looks too old for you."

"I'm in love with him," Sarah said to test the words and poured the mug full.

"Love?" said Edna.

Sarah took her coffee to the window and looked out at the highway. Jack had told her he was twenty-eight. It never occurred to her that he could be older. "What's taking them so long?" she said.

Edna laughed in a cruel way and Sarah walked over to the jukebox. "It's broke," said Edna.

Sarah read every song title, which took a while. Then she walked past the pocket knife display by the cash register and went into the ladies' room. It was the size of a closet and cold. The hot water tap was broken. She came back out and sat at the counter again.

"I have to start my vegetable soup," Edna said looking up at the clock.

"Is it homemade?" Sarah asked.

"Homemade out of a can," said Edna.

Maybe Jack had decided to take Connie with him and leave Sarah at the truck stop. She would have to take Connie's place and wear her uniform. She would have to get fat. Sarah thought she heard the bike in the distance and then she heard it. When they came in, the door slammed but Sarah didn't turn around.

"Here it is," Connie said.

The jacket was heavy on Sarah's shoulders. She looked down at the metal stars on the black leather. Laura wouldn't be caught dead in this jacket.

"So what do you think?" Connie said. "Does it fit?"

Sarah put her arms in the sleeves and zipped it up. "Are you sure you want to sell it?" she said. She felt uneasy in another woman's clothing.

"I think it would be best if me and that jacket parted company," said Connie. "I hope it brings you luck. It didn't me but that don't mean anything. Do you want the helmet too?"

Jack turned off the highway onto a county road. They drove through a town two blocks long with several empty buildings. Sarah felt sealed into the jacket and helmet. She could hardly bend her arms. The helmet had a dark visor. Jack slowed the bike and turned into the driveway of a small green house. He turned off the motor. He got off and started checking something on the motor.

"Don't you have anything better to do?" he asked because she was staring at him.

"No, I don't have anything better to do," she said.

"Take our stuff in the house," he said.

"I don't want to take our stuff in the house," she said watching his hands.

"We're only staying one night," he said. "Hand me my wrench." She handed it to him.

She was sitting on the back porch with the jacket on when Connie got home in her beat-up car. It was Indian summer.

"Aren't you warm in that jacket?" Connie asked. She had one foot on the bottom step.

"I'm fine," said Sarah. With the jacket on, she felt safe.

Connie came up the steps and looked at the geraniums on the porch rail in front of Sarah, making her move her feet. Then she went into the house. "Shit," she said when she got inside.

Sarah looked out at the shed at the end of the driveway. Beyond it was a dry cornfield. She used to hide in the cornfield across the gravel road from her grandfather Stockton's farm. The blades were green and sharp. She had thought she could hear conversation from inside the house, but she probably couldn't. Jack stood up. He rolled the motorcycle off the stand and started it. He listened to the motor then he turned it off and started adjusting it again. Sarah went inside.

"I wish I didn't have to work," Connie said. "My sister doesn't have to work." She pulled a frying pan from inside the oven. She was going to fry hamburger.

Sarah sat at the counter that separated the living room from the kitchen. She looked at the curtains on the window over the sink. They were bright orange. "Is your sister older or younger?" she asked.

"She's older."

"My sister is a twin," said Sarah.

"I always wanted a twin," Connie said. She salted the skillet. "Are you close?"

"Not anymore," Sarah said.

"I thought twins were supposed to be close," Connie said. She put the hamburger patties in the skillet and flattened them with a spatula. "What happened?"

"She got married," Sarah said.

Connie laughed. "Women lose interest in each other when they get married. Did you dress alike?"

"We dressed alike for fourteen years," said Sarah. They had their own language until they were four and called each other Sister. As soon as they started school, Irene said they had to call each other by their real names. That was when everything began to change.

"One thing you hate to do after working in a restaurant all day is cook," Connie said. The hamburger started to sizzle and she turned down the flame.

"Let me do it," Sarah said.

"You're a doll," Connie said in a cool voice.

Sarah got up and went around to the stove. She turned the hamburgers over and watched them fry. She remembered the first day she and Laura dressed differently. They were in the ninth grade. Laura wore red and she wore navy blue. She felt as if she were wearing almost nothing.

"She'll hear us," Sarah whispered. "I don't want her to hear us." She could see Connie listening for the sounds they were going to make. They were on the fold-out couch in the living room.

"She's not going to hear us," Jack said. He put his hand on her belly.

Footsteps moved across the ceiling. A door opened and

closed and footsteps came down the hallway, down the stairs, and into the living room, where they stopped. After a moment Connie shuffled across the linoleum into the kitchen. She opened a cupboard. She turned on the faucet and filled a glass with water. Then she left the kitchen and passed close to their bed on her way back upstairs. She seemed to be wearing only a thin nightgown.

"What does she want?" Sarah whispered.

"She wants to watch us make love," he said.

"Do you want her to watch?"

Jack said nothing.

Sarah lay on her back with the impression that she was not breathing. She felt as thin as paper. Her face was numb. "I can't sleep," she said. She threw off the cover and stood up. The linoleum was cold under her bare feet as she walked to the window. She looked out at the disappointing moon.

"Come to bed," Jack said from the dark. "I was just kidding."

"My sister told me I shouldn't come with you," Sarah said. She heard him yawn.

"Your sister's in on the conspiracy," he said.

"What conspiracy," she said to the cool night.

"You know. Don't be a dreamer. Passion is immoral. Come to bed."

The first thing Sarah saw the next morning was the top half of Connie over the counter. She had on her uniform and was making coffee. Jack was not in the bed.

"Morning," Connie said.

Sarah got out of bed without speaking and went to the bathroom. She shut the door. The door had no lock. She heard the back door slam and heavy footsteps come inside. Then she heard Jack's voice. Connie said something to him but Sarah couldn't understand what. She started to hurry. The back door slammed again and another man's voice shouted into the room. Something crashed. Sarah knew without ever having heard one that a fight had started. She opened the door. A big man in a cheap suit was going to punch Connie in the face.

"He's got a girl with him," Connie yelled.

"That don't mean anything," the man yelled back.

Jack grabbed the man by his sleeve and shoved him against the wall. The man was fat. A picture fell off the wall.

"Jesus Christ," Connie screamed at him.

Sarah came out of the bathroom.

"I told you he had a girl," Connie said. "They spent the night on my couch. She's an old friend of mine."

The man looked at Sarah.

"It's true," Sarah said. She felt calm telling a lie.

"I tried to tell you, you big asshole," Connie said.

The man walked over to the stove and poured himself a cup of coffee. He sat at the counter with it, holding the mug in one hand and staring out the window.

"You make me want to lead a clean life," Jack said in bed that night. He spoke in a soft voice. They were in a small motel outside Toledo. The bathroom had no door.

"What makes you say that?" Sarah asked listening hard. He rarely spoke in such a voice.

"You're good inside. Broads like Connie are a dime a dozen."

"I'm not good," said Sarah.

"Maybe you don't want to be good but you are," said Jack.

Sarah touched his shoulder. "You scared me last night," she said. "I thought you wanted to make love in front of her."

"I was testing you," he said. "You had the right reaction."

"Don't test me," she said.

"Don't worry. I wouldn't want anyone to watch us make love."

"Would you let someone watch you make love to another woman?" she asked.

"The important thing is I wouldn't do it with you."

"Jack," she said.

"I want us to find that island. We'll be the only people on it. We'll make love in the sand. We'll make love in the ocean."

"How is this going to happen?" Sarah asked. "We don't even know where it is."

"You have to believe in the dream before the dream can come true," Jack said. He slipped his hand over her belly. She put her arms around him.

"Do you want to make love now?" she whispered.

"No," he said. "I want to go to sleep feeling clean."

Seventeen

Sarah looked at the scarred pool table. The circle of light over it left the corners of the room in darkness. The place was chilly. When her turn came, she knocked in a ball then missed a ball. She stepped back to watch Jack. He hit in four balls in a row. Then the eight ball was the only one left on the table. He knocked it in.

"We'll play you a game of doubles," a man across the room said. He was playing darts with another man. They played a slow game, taking turns often.

Jack shook his head. He was in an unfriendly mood. He racked the balls.

"Let's play for a round of drinks," the man said. He looked at Sarah.

She shrugged and raised her glass too fast, spilling some beer. She chugged the rest. "Why not," she said.

They flipped a coin. The man lost.

"My name is Marty," he told her. He held his cigarette in his teeth and took aim. "That's Jimmy."

Marty broke and three balls went in. A surprise. Sarah looked at Jack.

"Whoa," Jack said. "You're too good for us." He put his hands up.

"Beginner's luck," said Marty. The ash fell off the end of his cigarette onto the table.

Sarah missed her shot then Jimmy put in several. Jack knocked in two and Marty finished up.

"Another game?" Marty said. He lit another cigarette in a furtive way.

"I can't do it boys," Jack said.

"Ten bucks," said Marty.

"Let's try," Sarah said to Jack. Jack was watching the television above the bar. "We can do better."

"I have an idea," Jimmy said scratching his head. Jimmy was stocky and nearly bald. He looked the meaner of the two. "How about you put up the girl?"

Sarah stopped breathing.

"What are you guys up to?" Jack said. He started to chew but he had no gum.

"What's she worth?" Jimmy asked.

"Worth more than you got," said Jack.

"Fifteen hundred?" Marty asked.

"More than that," Jack said.

"Fifteen is all we got," said Marty. "Just you and me'll play."

She said, "Jack."

Several people were watching them. All of a sudden Jack started chalking the tip of his cue. Jimmy pulled out a roll of bills. "Count it if you want," he said.

Jack counted it.

"He put up his woman," somebody said.

Marty grinned at Sarah. He winked. She felt as if she were standing across the room from herself. She had not taken off her jacket and now she zipped it up. The game started. She watched the blur of colors and listened to the hollow click of balls. Jack took a long time to pick his shots. Marty moved in fast.

Sarah put her hands in her pockets and ran out of the bar. From the side of the building she watched the highway. No cars were coming in the gray afternoon to take her away. She would have gone, she thought. She would have gone.

Then she saw Laura in a kitchen cutting open a cantaloupe, scooping out the seeds. Laura put the cantaloupe on a plate in front of Matthew. She was trying to make him happy. Why wasn't he happy?

No one was with Jack when he came out of the bar. He walked over to the bike, rolled it off its stand, and started it. He put his helmet on slowly. She ran toward him shouting his name. He seemed not to hear her. She grabbed his arm.

"Get on," he said.

"Did you get the money?" She got on behind him.

"I got it," he said.

"Were they pissed off?"

"Absolutely," he said.

"Thank goodness we never have to see those horrible people again," she said.

They pulled out of the parking lot.

"Why did you take the chance?" she shouted.

"I knew he would scratch," Jack said.

"He scratched?" she yelled. "What if he hadn't? What would I have done?"

"You would have gone with them," Jack yelled back. "That was the deal."

They went fast through the cold afternoon. They roared past a pickup truck. "You didn't have the right," Sarah shouted. She started pounding on his back. Jack pulled to the side of the road and turned off the motor. They got off the bike.

"Don't ever do that again." He pushed her. "Don't ever doubt my judgment."

"Was this another test?" she said. The pickup truck honked passing them now.

Jack grabbed her arm and pulled her close to him. She had never seen his eyes so hard. He clenched his teeth. "Learn to trust me," he said. "I know what I'm doing."

"I don't believe you," she said.

He pushed her arm behind her back and twisted it until she cried out, feeling nothing inside.

Unexpectedly they were racing through farmland that resembled Illinois. Plowed fields like corrugated paper went by. The flatness usually made her sleepy but now the flatness had speed. She felt she could go in any direction or change directions abruptly. Life seemed a well-lit place but it wasn't. They had been on the road twelve days and they were in Canada. She was cold all the time. Home was a place in the mirror. She saw Lloyd and Irene waiting at the end of their driveway. Laura stood beside them with her pinched look.

"Would you like some bread?" a little girl asked them in a roadside cafe. She was about six. She wore a long skirt and had brought them glasses of water. "The bread is homemade," she said. The place was overheated by a wood stove. The food contained no preservatives, a sign said. The poultry was raised on grain never sprayed with pesticides.

"Sure we would," Jack said. They were the only customers in the place.

The child walked carefully across the wooden floor to the glass case that displayed baked goods. She got out a small loaf of bread and brought it to them on a wooden board. Then she went back for a knife.

Sarah touched Jack's arm. He didn't flinch or draw in his breath. He did nothing but his whole body had a reaction. She pulled her hand back.

"You be careful when you carry that knife," he told the little girl. He began to cut the bread. She stood by their table and watched him. He looked at her. "You sure are pretty," he said.

Sarah saw her as a teenager with a sullen look, hitchhiking in jeans.

"Do you want something else?" the child asked.

"Yes, we do," Jack said.

"I'll get my mother," the child said and ran away.

"I told you my brother lives in Canada," Sarah said.

"So what," said Jack.

"He came up a year ago when he got drafted. It drives my dad crazy. My dad was a fighter pilot."

"What are you getting at?"

She wasn't sure she wanted to but she said, "Maybe we could go see my brother."

"I don't want to see your brother," said Jack.

"We probably couldn't find him anyway," she said.

"May I bring you some lunch?" the child's mother asked. She had a plump beauty. She wore a long skirt and a muslin blouse.

"I'll have the vegetable soup," Jack said staring at her blouse. "I'll bet it's homemade."

"Everything here is homemade," she said. "And for you?" she asked Sarah.

Jack watched the woman's hands, which she held carefully together. He watched her walk away.

"What are you thinking?" Sarah asked.

"I'd like to live a clean life," he said. "I'd like to have a family and live like these people."

"You'd get bored," Sarah said. "It wouldn't be enough for you."

"You don't know what I want," Jack said in a low voice. "You don't understand anything about me."

Sarah looked away. "This isn't my fault," she said. "You asked me to come with you. What am I supposed to do?"

Eighteen

"Did you used to be a jockey?" she asked the small man next to them. They were in the bar of a motel. She was on her second whiskey sour. On the bar were paper placemats with a map of the peninsula printed on them.

"I've spent some time at the track," the man said. He had large ears with hair growing out of them.

"I knew you had," she said. She looked at Jack. He was reading a road map of Canada.

"Harness racing," said the old man. He leaned back to get another look at her. "You're a pretty girl."

She saw Laura posing in a ruffled yellow dress for someone else's benefit. Sarah stood in her yellow dress and unmanageable hair next to Laura. They both carried white baskets with flower petals in them. A girl they didn't know was getting married and the sanctuary was hot. A fat man took their picture.

"Did you drive in any harness races?" she asked.

"No, I never did," he said.

"What use did you make of your size then?"

"You're pretty blunt," he said.

"I get blunt when I drink."

"My wife got blunt when she drank," he said. He scratched his nose.

Sarah looked at the couple with him. They weren't paying any attention to her. When she was with Laura, people paid attention to her.

"That's my daughter and her husband," he said. "We come here every Tuesday night. She knows the drummer."

"I'm a twin," Sarah said.

"Is your twin as pretty as you are?" he asked.

"My twin just got married," she said.

"Shorty," said the bartender. He made a circle with his finger and the old man nodded.

"It's cruel of him to call you Shorty," Sarah said.

"Everybody calls me Shorty," he said.

Sarah patted him on the shoulder. He was short and his daughter and son-in-law took him out on Tuesday night. His wife got blunt when she drank.

"Where'd you get your leather jacket?" Shorty asked.

"It's a long story."

"I ain't going nowhere," Shorty said. He looked harmless when he smiled.

"I envy your daughter," Sarah said.

Three musicians walked in. One of them sat down at the

organ and turned it on. Beside the organ was a potted tree. Then a woman in a shiny dress came in and started talking to the organist. The lights dimmed.

"Do you want to dance?" Sarah asked.

"You wouldn't want to dance with me," Shorty said.

Sarah tapped Jack on the shoulder. "This is Shorty," she said leaning back so they could see each other. "I want to dance with him."

The organist began to play "I'm in the Mood for Love." The woman began to sing.

"Be my guest," Jack said.

Dancing with him was like dancing with a child. Her arm went all the way around his shoulders. She saw them together, an old child and a girl in a black leather jacket, dancing.

"I met a girl like you once," he said. He held her closer. "If I had it to do again, I'd leave my wife."

"That's so sweet," she said.

"I didn't have the courage at the time," he said. "My wife's dead now."

"It's too bad you didn't leave her when you had the chance," Sarah said. "People should do things when they have the chance."

She felt close to Shorty. They danced for a long time. She felt close to the organist too, because he wouldn't stop looking at her.

She stood before the mirror in their room. Jack stood behind her. He looked at her in the mirror and pulled her tight against him. They watched each other in the mirror. He pulled at her clothes but he didn't pull them off. She started to unbutton her shirt but Jack ripped it open, watching himself in the mirror. He didn't take his eyes off himself as he unzipped his jeans. Then he held her jaw and made her watch them. He wouldn't let her turn her head away but held her stomach and breathed in her ear. They moved in a rhythm perfect for its wetness and its sting. She watched the frank expression on her face and couldn't believe that her face looked beautiful. She had never felt such hunger.

"You make me want to live a clean life," Jack whispered in an urgent voice. He dug his fingers into her stomach.

In bed she felt the lightness of the hair on his leg against hers for one peaceful moment. She must have slept. The next moment she was listening to the zipper of his pack in the dark. He moved, his clothes whispering in the room, and stood by her head for a long time. She was afraid. Then the door opened and clicked shut. She heard the light crunch of gravel outside as he rolled his bike toward the road. The motor started and roared into the distance. Then there was silence.

"Is everything okay in there?" a woman's voice called.

Sarah sat up. She was sweating. It was noon.

"Do you need help?" the voice said.

Sarah pulled on her jeans and her ripped shirt. She opened the door. The woman stepped back.

"I didn't know it was so late," Sarah whispered squinting at the light.

"I have to clean the room," the woman said. She stared at Sarah's shirt.

Sarah closed the door and went into the bathroom. She looked at herself in the mirror. Her grandmother's nose was there and the Broderhouse eyes. Her head ached and her face was swollen. Sarah slapped the right cheek. She slapped it harder. Then she slapped it again and again as hard as she dared but it was never hard enough. She slapped the other cheek and made the face have no expression. She made the eyes have no tears. The lavatory had rust stains in it. She could smell iron in the water. She drank water out of her hands and tasted it.

Nineteen

Behind her the street was quiet. She stood on the wide front porch of an old farmhouse in a small town in Michigan. The lace curtains were drawn and there were no sounds from the house. By the door hung a sign FURNISHED APARTMENTS FOR RENT.

"Where in the hell did you come from?" an old man said. He was leaning on crutches behind the screen door.

Sarah told him a lie.

"Do you have a job?" he asked.

She did. She was going to be a waitress at the Fish House. He opened the door and she followed him into the foyer. On the left were French doors. On the right was an ordinary door with the number one above it.

"Who is it, Kenneth?" a voice called.

They went into the room behind the French doors. A woman stood next to an upright piano clutching the pearls at her throat. She wore thick glasses.

"I'm going to show her number three," he said.

"Number three is nice," said the woman. She looked at the floor lamp next to Sarah. "From the bedroom window you can see my rose garden."

"Number three has the television," said the old man.

"That's a beautiful piano," Sarah said. "Do you play?"

"I went to Juilliard when I was a girl," the woman said. "I was nearly a concert pianist."

"My sister and I took piano lessons for years," Sarah said. All at once she missed Laura. "We played duets constantly."

"Isn't that nice?" said the woman. "I used to give lessons. I was the organist at the church up the street. You passed it on your way here."

She was nearly blind. She had nearly been a concert pianist.

"I was a contractor in Jersey," said the old man. "You think you'll go back but you never do."

"My family lives in New Jersey," said the old woman.

"Most of her family is dead," the old man said.

Sarah was watching television when someone tapped on her door. She turned the television off and listened to the old man's wife playing *Clair de Lune* on the piano downstairs. Either she or Laura had played *Clair de Lune* when they were kids. She couldn't remember who.

"Who is it?" she called.

"Let me in quick," a woman's voice said.

Sarah opened the door. A woman in a miniskirt and dyed black hair slipped inside. "Hide me," she said.

Sarah followed the woman through the apartment. If Laura could see the lavender outfit, she would laugh. Sarah felt Laura's laughter on her mouth.

"He's going to beat me up," the woman said in a southern accent. "Hide me in your shower."

"Maybe I should call the police," Sarah said.

"No," the woman cried. She took hold of Sarah's arm. Her fingers were strong. "He'll kill me. You don't know him."

Sarah put her hand over the woman's and was startled by the soft, cool skin.

"Don't leave me," the woman said. She went into the bathroom and got into the metal shower stall. She pulled the shower curtain shut.

Sarah leaned against the bathroom wall. She looked at the pink toilet paper and the pink curtains. She looked at the yellow wallpaper.

"He'll say it's my fault," the woman said behind the curtain. She started to cry.

"I'm sure it isn't your fault," Sarah said.

"Everything is my fault."

"That can't be true," Sarah said.

"Just when things get smoothed out, something else goes wrong. In Texas he worked in an ammunition factory. I had a job as a maid but I got pregnant. So whose fault was it?"

"Did he think he had nothing to do with it?"

"I didn't want to but I got an abortion."

"Why don't you leave him?" Sarah asked. She sat on the floor outside the shower stall.

"I can't leave him," the woman said. "He needs me."

Now someone else was beating on Sarah's door.

"It's him. It's him," the woman cried. "Don't let him in."

"I'm just going to see who it is," Sarah said. She got up and went out into the living room.

"Police," a man's voice said.

She opened the door. Beside the policeman stood a tall man with his hands behind his back.

"We're looking for his wife," said the policeman.

Sarah opened her mouth then she closed it. The man reminded her of Ralph Timbley. The Timbleys were their only neighbors. It was in the early fifties and they had just moved to the farm. Ralph Timbley had his feet in the air when they walked into his house. He got out of his recliner and shook hands, backing away from Lloyd. Everybody sat down facing the Timbleys' new television and tried to make out what was happening. The living room floor was on a slant.

"We want to make sure she's okay," the officer told Sarah.

"You won't let him hurt her?" she said.

Lloyd didn't tell them until years later about the night Helen Timbley called and said Ralph was trying to kill her. Irene was in town playing bridge. Lloyd told the kids not to move from the couch and drove down to save Helen. He said his knees were black and blue from getting knocked on the floor. Finally Ralph fell against the door jamb and knocked himself out he was so drunk.

Sarah glanced at the tall man at her door. He was staring

at her shoes. He had bad posture but he was nice looking. Ralph Timbley was a nice looking man always in need of a shave. Or love, Sarah thought when she was old enough. His wife even waited on their three boys.

"Beatrice," the man called. "It's me, sugar." His face was so pale.

Sarah went back into the bathroom and pulled open the shower curtain. Beatrice was crouched in a corner. She had the skinny white legs of a young girl.

"I won't come out as long as he's drunk," she whispered. "No matter what he says, he'll beat me up again. He tries to kill me all the time."

"A policeman is here," Sarah said.

Beatrice started crying again. "Then we'll both go to jail," she said. "Just like the last time."

Sarah knelt in the shower and put her arm around Beatrice. She was thin for a woman with so much hair. Sarah wanted to take her in. They would be companions. She saw them living together, the small woman in her lavender outfit and Sarah in her black leather jacket, watching television on the vinyl couch.

Twenty

Opera music was coming up through the living room floor. Sarah walked into her bedroom but she could hear it even louder in there. She did not want to live with opera music coming up through her floor.

"I'm sorry to bother you," she said when the new tenant opened the door to number one. He opened it only a few inches as if someone were naked in the room behind him. He wore rimless glasses. She laughed apologetically.

"Come in," he said. There was no furniture, only large pillows on the floor of the living room and lots of cardboard boxes. The young man was wearing a black kimono with a red sash. He was short and square, not someone her mother would choose. His face was terribly round.

"I'm trying to lose weight," he said. "I want to get down to my old wrestling weight."

"Why?"

"I just want to see if I can do it," he said. "Do you like opera?"

"I never listened to opera until today," she said.

"You should listen to opera," he said. He looked at one of the boxes. "Books. I teach at the junior college." He looked at her. His eyes were blue. "English."

"I see," she said.

"Would you like some tea?"

While he was in the kitchen, Sarah decided she would tell him as soon as he came back. She wanted him to understand that when his music came up through her floor, she felt invaded. She was forced to listen to it and she couldn't concentrate on anything else.

"This is my favorite aria," he said coming back into the living room. He carried a tray with an Oriental teapot and cups on it. He set it on the floor and bowed. Then he sat on the floor. She believed he was sitting in the lotus position. She heard herself say to Laura, *he was sitting in the lotus position.*

"I should probably listen to opera more often," Sarah said, "but I have always had the impression that opera singers are straining themselves."

"Sometimes when I hear Wagner, I tremble," the man said with his eyes closed.

He trembles when he hears Wagner, she told Laura.

They drank tea and listened to the music for some time.

When it was over she said, "Thank you for playing your records for me."

"What do you do in life?" he asked.

"I'm a photographer," she said. "At the moment I'm working as a waitress."

"Where is your camera?" he asked.

"I don't have it with me," she said. "I was traveling by motorcycle and there wasn't room."

"Do they have vegetarian food where you work?" he asked.

"They have fish," she said standing.

"I'll have dinner there tomorrow. My name is Timothy."

"Tomorrow is my day off." Sarah looked at the ceiling. She looked at the telephone on the floor and followed the wire along the baseboard to the wall jack. She studied where the wire went into the jack. "Would you like to have dinner at my apartment tomorrow night?" she asked.

Laura would never ask such a person to dinner.

"Dear," the old woman whispered from the French doors as Sarah left number one. "Are you going to the drugstore by any chance? I need something and he won't get it for me."

Sarah stepped inside the old people's apartment. The woman smelled of must and lavender.

"Alice," he called from the other room. "What are you doing in there Alice?"

"Ask the druggist to refill my prescription," she said quickly. "He'll know which one."

The old man's steps came slowly into the room. "Here now," he said to his wife.

"I'm in pain," said Alice.

"I told you I would go to the drugstore later and I will. Don't pay any attention to her," he said to Sarah. "Say. I wanted to tell you. There won't be any more trouble from now on. I told those people they had to move out."

"What will happen to them?" Sarah asked. "Where will they go?"

"I suspect they'll be going back to Georgia," he said. "You think you know who you're renting to but you never do." Sarah saw them driving south in an old Buick, the backseat full of clothes. On top of everything was a lamp.

She left the house and started toward town. She was going to the grocery store. She walked along the sidewalk and stopped in front of a yellow frame house. A cat was stalking a bird in the yard. She clapped her hands and the bird flew away. The cat stepped on a flower.

A small church was just ahead. It looked as if it belonged in a place with no trees. She didn't want to go inside but she crossed the street and went in. As a kid she had made herself sit up straight on the hard pews and pay attention to the organ music. She watched Jesus in the stained-glass window, pale like a man with no personality, holding a white lamb. Dirty thoughts kept popping into her mind. She stole fifteen cents from the collection plate.

Now she wanted to get out of the church fast. But first she felt she must memorize the place. She saw a table with messy candles on it and a shaft of light coming in through a high window. She saw wilted flowers in a jar on the floor beside the altar. Then she rushed outside into the clean and spacious air. She was going to the grocery store. She was going to put her life in order. Order seemed shaped like an egg.

Timothy was already sitting on her floor in the lotus position when someone else knocked.

"That must be Vern," she said and opened the door.

The small immaculate man who washed dishes at the Fish House handed her flowers. He wore a white shirt open at the neck and a gold chain.

"In love is where I yearn to be," he said. "Love is bondage, the cell mate's key. Locked up together, we are free. In love is where I yearn to be."

"That's beautiful, Vern," she said.

Vern touched his dark hair. His hair was a toupee.

"I want you to meet Timothy," she said opening the door wider. These men, this place seemed to have nothing to do with her.

"I'm sorry," said Vern.

"How you doing, Vern?" Timothy said. He didn't get up.

"I thought I was to be the only guest," Vern said. He stayed outside on the landing.

"It was a last minute thing," Sarah said. "Timothy just moved in downstairs." She reached out to touch Vern's arm but he drew away. He stared at her.

"Pretty girls are all alike," he said. "Pretty girls never mean what they say." He started down the stairs.

"I meant it," Sarah called after him. She heard the front door open and close quietly.

"What did you tell him?" Timothy asked.

"I told him I would fix him dinner on his birthday," Sarah said. She closed the door and leaned against it.

"Then you shouldn't have invited me," said Timothy.

"I didn't really want to be with him," she said. "But he seemed to like me so much, I thought I should pay attention to him."

"Do you pay attention to everyone who seems to like you?" Timothy asked.

"Don't you?" she said.

"He's in love with you," said Timothy. "He'll never forgive you."

Twenty-one

Sunday morning the restaurant was full of families eating pancakes on tables covered with white paper. A girl and her mother were talking in shrill voices. Sarah walked toward a man sitting alone at a table for two by the window. He sat very straight in his business suit. He was looking out the window. She said good morning.

He looked at her. "Nurse," he said. He put his hand over his heart. "Bring me tomato juice and coffee."

"If you have a hangover you should eat scrambled eggs and toast," she said. She studied the shiny fabric of his suit.

"Bring me that," he said.

He was the best looking man she had ever seen but he only had one arm.

"Scramble me two eggs light," she told the breakfast cook.

Martha laughed. "You'll get them however they turn out," she said.

"Why aren't you ever nice?" Sarah asked. She put two slices of bread in the toaster. She pushed the bread down.

"I'll tell you why," Martha said through her nose, her breasts jiggling as she worked. "The world ain't a nice place." She shoved the plate onto the counter under the infrared lights.

The toast popped up and Sarah pushed it down again as Vern walked by. "Hi Vern," she said without looking at him. She always spoke to him but he never answered. He was never going to forgive her. The toast popped up again. "Why doesn't somebody fix this toaster," she said.

She buttered the toast and put it on the plate. She carried the plate out into the dining room.

The man with one arm looked at the eggs. He looked at her. "You saved my life. I think I'm in love with you," he said.

She watched him take a careful bite of toast, leaning forward as if he might lose his balance.

"I'll leave you now," Sarah said. She shoved her hands into her apron pockets.

"Don't leave," he said. He put the toast down and wiped his mouth with the paper napkin.

She heard the little girl ask in her shrill voice for more syrup and she said, "I have to get back to work."

"Could I see you later?" He put the napkin back on his lap. Of course he had to do everything with one hand.

"I'll have to think about it," she said. She had never gotten picked up by a customer.

"Is this the only restaurant in town?" he asked.

"There's an Italian restaurant on the lake."

"Let's go there," he said.

"I guess that would be all right," she said. He was so handsome.

We don't know anything about him, her father said. *He has one arm*, she told him.

"I just told that man I would go out with him," Sarah said to Hazel by the coffeepot. Hazel was the waitress who had been there the longest. She was bitter about her ex-husband. She inhaled cigarette smoke through her nose.

Hazel looked across the room. "Dick?" she said.

That Hazel knew Dick made him seem less interesting.

"He comes through every few weeks. He must be a traveling salesman," Hazel said.

"A traveling salesman," said Sarah.

Hazel picked up the coffeepot and walked away.

He's a traveling salesman with one arm, Sarah told her father.

She was glad he didn't pin up the sleeve of his sweater or tuck it into his waistband. He stood on the landing, shorter than she had expected, with a bottle of scotch in his hand. It was an expensive brand. She didn't want to but she looked at his empty sleeve.

"I need a drink," he said. He followed her into the kitchen. She got out ice cubes and poured scotch into two glasses. He put his arm around her waist. She held the glasses of scotch between them as he leaned forward and kissed her hard.

"What's the matter?" he asked.

She didn't know she was going to say it. "I've never been kissed by a man with one arm before."

He blinked. "I can do everything I need to do," he said.

"How did it happen?"

"In a hunting accident when I was eleven," he said.

"Oh God I'm sorry," she said. He had been a teenager with one arm. Now he was a young man with one arm.

He got out a pack of cigarettes and shook one up. He offered it to her but she said no. He put it in his mouth and pulled a pack of matches out of his pocket. He struck the match without removing it from the pack, then lit the cigarette and waved the match out. He took a glass from her and went into the living room. He sat on the vinyl couch.

"I apologize for asking," Sarah said sitting next to him.

"Don't apologize," he said. "Don't ever apologize for saying what you're thinking. Now sit on the other side so I can put my arm around you."

The restaurant was called Little Venice. The tables had red-and-white tablecloths and a violinist was playing in the middle of the room. Dick opened the menu.

"What looks good?" he asked.

"I've never been here before," she said. She hoped the violinist wouldn't come play at their table.

"Let's have spaghetti. You can't miss with spaghetti," Dick said.

"Can you manage spaghetti?" she asked and looked all around his face.

He laughed. When he laughed, his whole face changed. "Of course I can manage spaghetti," he said.

"You have a good sense of humor," she said.

"I try to have a good time," he said.

"That's what my sister does," said Sarah. She wasn't going to tell him Laura was her twin.

"What else is there to do in life?" he asked.

"You can be unhappy," she said. "You can have a lot of worries."

He put his hand over hers. "Are you unhappy?"

She looked at the violinist. He was playing a sad melody. Behind him were the lighted signs for the rest rooms. A man dressed in black had just come out of the men's room.

"What's wrong," Dick said.

"I don't believe this," she said. "My old boyfriend is here. I haven't seen him in weeks."

"We can leave if you want," said Dick. "Say the word."

"I don't want to leave," she said. Jack was coming toward them. The violinist finished his song.

"Then we won't leave."

"Jack," she said, "this is Dick. Dick, Jack."

Dick didn't stand up. He didn't offer his hand.

"Come over here and talk to me," said Jack.

"The lady is with me," Dick said.

"You can have her right back," Jack said in an irritable voice.

"It's okay," she said to Dick. She got up and walked away from the table with Jack.

"How did you find me?" she asked.

He grinned. "I want you to walk out of here with me right now."

"You left me stranded in Canada. I had to hitch a ride with a truck driver."

They were standing next to the rest rooms. She had to strain to hear him he was talking so low. "I'm going to find that island," he said. "I want you to come with me."

"I won't do it," she said.

"You're making a big mistake," he said.

She went into the ladies' room. She locked herself inside one of the stalls. Maybe Jack was right. Maybe it was a mistake for her not to go. She heard the outside door open.

"Don't come near me," she said.

"All you have to do is walk out of here with me and I won't hurt you. Are you going to walk out of here with me?" Jack said.

"No," she said.

Jack kicked open the stall door. "You really are stupid," he said.

The door opened behind him and a woman walked in. She stepped aside as he walked out.

"Are you okay honey?" she asked. "Your friend asked me to check on you."

Sarah came out of the stall. The woman wore a lot of makeup and her perfume was strong. She had an enormous bosom and plump, comforting arms.

Twenty-two

She ate some yogurt. She ate some raisins and turned on the six o'clock news. She was waiting for a knock on her door. *Please, please leave me alone,* she would say. If he wouldn't go away, she was supposed to stomp on the floor three times and Timothy would come up. Dick had made this arrangement before leaving for Saginaw. She listened to the opera music through the floor. She was beginning to like opera music.

At six-thirty the knock came. She had told herself that she wasn't going to open the door but she opened it. Jack put his foot in the doorway. He filled the doorway. Sarah stepped back and he entered her apartment. He was wearing new black leather pants. She smelled the leather. She smelled his sweat. She did not stomp on the floor.

"Close those blinds," he said. He sat on the couch and rubbed the back of his neck.

Sarah pulled the venetian blinds shut.

"Sit down," he said. He looked her over and grinned as if someday she might figure it all out. "I need to stay here a few days," he said. "I don't know why the police want to talk to me but they do."

"What did you do?"

"I hit a car. Nobody was hurt," he said. He pulled a gun out of his pocket.

"Where did you get that?" she said. "Be careful where you point it."

"Get me a candle. Do you have a candle?"

Yes she had a candle. Sometimes she ate dinner by candlelight to keep away the loneliness. She went into the kitchen and imagined herself climbing out the bathroom window. She hunted for the candle. She found it in a drawer and took it back into the living room. Jack lit the candle and set it on the coffee table next to the gun.

"Is it loaded?" she asked.

"Why would I carry an empty gun?" he said.

"Is the safety on?" she asked. "Put the safety on."

"For Christ sake," he said and put the gun back in his pocket.

The first time he hurt her was toward the end of summer. They were playing pool in a bar up at the lake. They were running out of money. She didn't know why she did it but she bought a pack of cigarettes out of a vending machine. She wasn't a smoker. She was about to light one when Jack came over and shoved the cigarette into her mouth. "We don't have money to waste on cigarettes," he said. She spit the tobacco into a napkin.

"Why do you let him treat you that way?" the bartender asked after Jack went away.

"I'm in love with him," she said.

The bartender shook his head in disgust. She thought he was disgusted with her. Maybe he was. Jack had already said he thought women who smoked cigarettes looked like sluts.

Jack blew out the candle and looked at her sideways. He turned his head and looked at her from every angle. "Don't move," he said.

She looked down at herself.

"You're pregnant."

"Stop it," she said.

"I have willed it. My sperm are inside you. It's too late."

She stared at him. What he was saying did not seem impossible.

"Make love to me," he said.

"No," she said. "You're scaring me."

Jack reached across the table and took her arm. He stood and came around to her. He unbuckled his belt and unzipped his leather pants.

"Take them off," he said. He meant her jeans.

She slipped off her jeans. Jack pushed her onto the floor. She closed her eyes and listened to the opera music below. He held her shoulders and pressed them against the floor. The bones of her spine burned against the hard rug. She braced her feet. Her head ached and she felt thirsty. She thought he would never stop. He stopped.

"That's never happened to me before," he said. He got off her and zipped up his pants. He walked to the window.

Sarah pulled her jeans back on.

"You aren't expecting anyone, are you?" he said, pushing the curtain aside. He stepped over to the television. Her purse was on top of the television.

"Don't," she said. "It's all the money I have." She knelt by the coffee table and watched him dig around in her purse.

He took her money and stuffed it into his pocket. "I'm leaving," he said. "You'll never see me again. Someday you'll be sorry."

"I'll never be sorry," she said.

Jack stood in front of the door with his back to her so she got a good look at it. Then he opened the door and walked out. She closed her eyes and listened to the room. She felt nothing inside but emptiness. And outside there was nothing that mattered to her. Then she knew she was satisfied.

"Dad," she said into the phone. She was in the booth outside the drugstore. It was dark. She barely let the receiver touch her ear. She didn't let the mouthpiece touch her mouth.

"Sister," he said. "Where are you honey?"

His voice filled her. At last she started to cry.

"I want to come home," she said.

"Are you okay?" he said.

"I'm okay."

"Tell us where to come get you," he said.

"I want to take the bus home," she said. "Can you send me some money?"

"Let us come get you."

An extension was picked up. "Where are you?" Laura asked.

"In Michigan," Sarah said.

"It's Sarah," Lloyd shouted into the background.

"Are you pregnant?" Laura asked.

"Christ," said Sarah.

Another phone was picked up. "Hi honey," her mother said in a hurt voice. Sarah felt wrapped in the voice.

"I'm sorry Mother," she said. She started to cry again.

"Are you coming home?" Irene asked.

A car went by and honked. Someone in the car looked at her in the lighted phone booth. Sarah pressed the palm of one hand against the glass door without opening it. Was she on the inside looking out at the world? Or was she on the outside looking in?

"I can drive up and get you," Laura said.

"I want to take the bus," Sarah said. She knew that she must take the bus.

"Are you all right?" Irene asked.

"I can't hear you very well," Sarah said.

"We're so happy you're coming home," said Lloyd.

"We had to move your things out of the apartment," Laura said. "Since no one knew when you were coming home."

"You can stay here as long as you want," Lloyd was saying. "You can have your old room. We love you Sister."

"I love you too," Sarah said.

"Tell me where to send the money," Lloyd said. "I'll wire it first thing in the morning."

Sarah gave them the Fish House address. She saw Laura walk into the dining room wearing a black leather coat and tall boots. Behind her were two men dressed as waiters. Sarah ran into the kitchen.

"Hide in the freezer," the cook shouted behind the grill.

"You're judging me," Sarah said.

"Nobody's judging you," said Irene. She was garnishing salads.

"Love is bondage," Vern said. "You're not free." He touched his hair, then pulled it off his head. He held it out to her like a gift.

Twenty-three

"You've gained weight," Laura said.

"I only gained seven pounds," said Sarah.

They were in Laura's car. Laura had shown up instead of the money. She sat at the wheel in neat slacks and a pull-over. Sarah sat on the passenger side in jeans and her black leather jacket. She felt fat and her few possessions were in the backseat.

"Seven pounds isn't that much," she said.

"I think you'd feel better if you lost weight. I always do," Laura said in a helpful voice.

Sarah listened to the quiet engine. She listened to the clock ticking. She hadn't even been able to get angry that Laura had come. She only felt helpless.

"Are you letting your hair grow?" Laura asked and turned on the radio.

"I haven't been able to afford a haircut lately."

"We've never looked good in long hair," said Laura. She turned onto the highway going south toward Ohio. It was the same highway Sarah and Jack had traveled coming north. Laura accelerated past a semitrailer truck.

"I think it depends on the style," Sarah said.

"No. We just don't look good in long hair," said Laura.

They had long hair when they were fourteen. Irene got disgusted with it and cut it off the day of their first boy-girl party. She insisted that Sarah wear her black suede correction shoes that night. "The more you wear them," Irene said, "the sooner you can stop wearing them." Laura never had to wear correction shoes.

"What a depressing day," Laura said. She looked out at the Michigan landscape and sighed.

Sarah watched an old cornfield go by. When they had gotten to the party, some kids were already playing spin the bottle in the basement. "We shouldn't stay at a party where this game is being played," she told Laura. She was in her religious phase at the time. "Why not?" Laura wanted to know.

Nathan Brown gave the bottle a spin. He was tall and blond and the cutest boy in ninth grade. If the bottle landed on her, Sarah thought, the boys would groan. *Please let it land on me*, she prayed. It did. She walked in agony into the dark pantry in her short hair and heavy black suede correction shoes and the gray wool jumper she thought made her look fat. In the background the phonograph began to play "Where Are You, Little Star?"

"We don't have to if you don't want," she told Nathan. She would understand if he didn't want to kiss her. She hunted for his blue eyes in the dark. His breathing was too loud. She felt it on her left eyelid just before he kissed the side of her nose. His hand touched her breast. She stared at the bright line of light under the door. Outside the kids started shouting and clapping. Someone beat on the door. When they came out, Nathan asked Laura to dance.

A light snow had begun to fall on the cornfield. Soon it would be Thanksgiving. Sarah felt nostalgic for the fireplace in the farmhouse where they used to live. On the mantle was a small brown radio.

"Mother and Dad are so relieved you're coming home. They've been worried sick," Laura said.

"Everybody's always worried sick about somebody," said Sarah.

"What did you expect?" Laura asked. "You disappeared. Dad was going to call the police until I told him what happened."

"What did you tell him?" Sarah asked.

"They couldn't believe you did it. Everybody has been talking about you," Laura said.

"What have they been saying?"

"They just want you back to the way you were before."

"I wasn't happy before," said Sarah.

"Of course you were happy. You were even sweet and funny when you wanted to be."

Sarah zipped up her jacket.

"Why are you wearing that ugly jacket? Why don't you wear makeup anymore?" Laura asked.

"This is what I feel like wearing," said Sarah.

"Then I would hate to be in your shoes. You must feel awful."

"I don't feel awful," Sarah said. She smiled at her sister. She didn't feel much of anything.

"Why can't you be yourself?" Laura asked like a complaint.

"Just be yourself," Irene used to say in an easy tone of voice. Sarah thought she meant be ordinary. Be good. Cross your ankles not your knees.

"I am myself," Sarah said. "Maybe you don't recognize me."

"I disagree," said Laura. "I think you should stop trying to look so tough."

"What am I supposed to look like?" Sarah asked.

"Why don't you dress like a normal person? Maybe something feminine."

Sarah laughed. "When you're traveling on a motorcycle, this is normal," she said.

"You aren't traveling on a motorcycle anymore," Laura said. "You don't belong on a motorcycle."

"Where do I belong?"

"Not on a motorcycle."

"You don't know where I belong," Sarah said. "You don't even know me."

Twenty-four

"I want to go home but they won't let me," Myrtie said. Her face seemed about to change. The expression was familiar but she had lost weight. She wore a pillbox hat and a purple cardigan upside down.

Sarah knelt by her chair. It was the Early American chair in Peter's old room. "At least you're not lonely here," she said.

"Yes I am," said her grandmother.

"I know what you mean," said Sarah.

"I left some things over there that I have to have." Myrtie looked sly. She'd escaped twice already.

"What things?" Sarah asked.

"She won't let me watch television," said Myrtie.

"Too much television isn't good for you Grandmother,"

said Sarah. "But what the heck at your age." She touched her grandmother's hand. The skin was dry and papery.

"I like my little house better," Myrtie said. She clasped her hands in a worried way.

"I know," said Sarah. "But you left the gas stove on twice."

"I wish Boyd Michaels was here," Myrtie said and closed her eyes.

"What happened to Boyd Michaels?" Sarah asked.

"He and Ethel were transferred to Evansville. I surely miss them," she said. After Reverend Michaels got transferred, the only men left in her life were her sons and Jesus.

Sarah went to the window but she didn't look out. She was thinking of a picture of her grandmother at seventeen, sitting on her father's knee. Myrtie and her father looked out at the camera as if they were strangers to each other.

"'Lo! I tell you a mystery,'" Myrtie said. "'We shall not all sleep, but we shall all be changed, in a moment, in the twinkling of an eye, at the last trumpet.'"

Sarah looked out the window. It had begun to snow.

"'Death is swallowed up in victory. O death, where is thy victory? O death, where is thy sting?'"

"It's snowing Grandmother," said Sarah.

"'The sting of death is sin, and the power of sin is the law,'" Myrtie said with emotion. "'But thanks be to God, who gives us the victory through our Lord Jesus Christ.'"

A woman had stood up in Myrtie's church at a Wednesday night prayer meeting and confessed that she'd been going out and doing things she shouldn't. Sarah was six at the time and wondered, what things?

Myrtie stood up and dragged her slippers across the carpet. She touched the wallpaper. "Someday we're going to leave these old mortal bodies behind," she said. "Oh what a glorious day that will be."

"You've been looking forward to it for a long time, haven't you?" Sarah said.

"I surely have."

"Can I get you anything Grandmother?" Sarah asked.

"I could eat a dish of ice cream."

"She's already had ice cream today," Irene said in the kitchen. She was weeding out her recipe file.

"Who cares," Sarah said. "She's old and unhappy. Let her eat ice cream." She opened the freezer and stood in the chill. She looked at the frozen meat, the frozen vegetables, the ice cubes.

"She needs nutritious food," said Irene.

"I'll put some banana on it."

"I don't know what I'm going to do with you," Myrtie said coming into the kitchen.

"I'm not Ansel, Mother," Lloyd said close behind her. "Watch your feet."

"Oh yes you are." She shook her finger at Irene. "He thinks he can fool me."

Lloyd and Irene looked at each other.

"What are you two up to?" Myrtie asked.

Sarah scooped some vanilla ice cream out into a dish.

"This is my wife, Irene. I'm your son, Lloyd." He looked shaken.

"This is some woman I don't know anything about, Ansel." Myrtie raised her chin and looked out the window.

"I'm going to give her a whole one this time," Lloyd said.

"Don't give her too much," said Irene.

"I want to know what's going on here," Myrtie said to her. Her voice sounded mean but she looked scared.

"Calm down," said Irene. She pulled a chair out for Myrtie.

"I'm not going to calm down," Myrtie said as she sat. She pulled her sweater closer around her.

"Why don't we put that on right," Irene said.

"Don't touch me," said Myrtie.

Lloyd mashed a tranquilizer into a bite of banana and brought it over to Myrtie.

"She said she needed some things," said Sarah. "What things?"

"She's been talking about fishing," Lloyd said. "I expect she wants Dad's fishing stool." He gave her the bite of banana and held her chin while she swallowed.

Myrtie shrugged and smiled at him. "You look sweet enough to eat," she said.

Sarah walked her grandmother back through the house. She listened to the shuffling of Myrtie's slippers on the hardwood floor. She looked at the family pictures on the wall in the hallway. Irene called it her rogues' gallery. Sarah saw herself alone at the end of the row, dressed in her leather jacket, leaning against a brick wall.

"I believe you're as tall as I am now," Myrtie said. She shrugged and smiled. Everything was helpless.

"I've grown up," Sarah said.

"I know I've gotten shorter," said Myrtie.

Sarah helped her undress and put on her nightgown. She

hadn't seen her grandmother's body in years. She remembered feeling smothered by her bosom in a room with a sewing machine, but Myrtie had almost no breasts left. Myrtie got into bed and lay staring at nothing, not even the ceiling.

"Good night Grandmother," Sarah said. She held Myrtie's heart-shaped old face in her hands.

"Good night, honey," Myrtie said.

"I love you." Sarah kissed her cheek, her mouth.

"'Do not be deceived,'" said Myrtie. "'Bad company ruins good morals. Come to your right mind, and sin no more. For some have no knowledge of God. I say this to your shame.'"

Sarah saw a woman look out a window with no curtains and then put a cross in the window where her face had been.

"I know, Grandmother."

Twenty-five

Kevin's bedroom door was open. The woman in bed with him had red hair that lay on the pillow like a wig. His leg was on top of the wool blanket and his arm was flung over his forehead. Parts of them lay everywhere, like violence. Sarah hadn't seen him since the day he showed her his new sculpture. She watched him as if he were dead.

She watched the November day from his kitchen window. It was raining. It was seven o'clock in the morning. She opened the wood stove and put dry leaves and kindling inside. She lit the leaves, watched the kindling begin to burn, then added larger pieces of wood.

"Help me," she whispered to the flames. "Help me."

"Sarah," Kevin said behind her.

She closed the stove and remained kneeling before it.

The floor was cold through her jeans. She wanted Kevin to pull her up and hold her. She wanted to lay her ear against his chest and listen to his heart.

"Where have you been?" he asked.

She stood and turned to him. He jammed his hands into the pockets of his jeans.

"Where did you get that great jacket?" he said.

"In my travels," she said.

"I need coffee," he said. He carried the kettle to the sink. Sarah listened to the hollow sound diminish as the kettle filled. She watched him put the kettle on the stove.

"I wish I'd found you alone waiting for me," she said.

He grinned and tossed a champagne bottle into the garbage can. Then he got two cups out of the cupboard. He put two teaspoons of instant coffee into the cups.

"What happened to the eggshells?" she asked. "What happened to the cheesecloth?" She wanted him to talk about love the way he did before.

"Eggshells are a lot of trouble," he said.

"Your life has changed," she said.

He shrugged.

"I went to Canada with a man on a motorcycle. I was afraid I was going to miss something."

Kevin laughed. "Maybe you were right."

"He left me and I hitchhiked to Michigan. I worked in a restaurant there."

"That took guts," Kevin said.

"Maybe it didn't," she said. "Maybe I was only running away."

"Maybe you needed to run away to find what you were looking for," he said.

"What was I looking for?" she asked.

She went to him and he put his arms around her. She stayed in his arms for a long time, breathing in the clean smell of his shirt. She heard the other woman walk in. Kevin whispered something and the woman went away.

"Was that you I heard coming in at dawn?" Irene asked. She was sitting with her arms on the kitchen table. She folded her hands before her. Her hands looked stiff and wounded.

"I wasn't coming in. I was leaving," Sarah said. "I couldn't sleep. I drove around and then I went out to see Kevin."

"Why he probably wasn't even up at that hour."

Sarah looked out the window at the trees in the ravine behind the house. They had no leaves. Their dark arms were misshapen against the sky.

"You're right. He was in bed with a woman."

Irene sighed. "It may seem silly to you but your father and I have certain standards. We've lived in this town all our lives."

"What does that have to do with me?" She knew what it had to do with her.

"As long as you live in this house, we expect you to respect our standards. We can't have you coming and going at dawn."

"You don't understand," said Sarah.

"What don't I understand?"

Sarah looked at the room. Everything was in order.

"I traveled with Jack. We stayed together in motels."

Irene touched her forehead. "You didn't have to tell me that," she said.

"You might as well know the truth," Sarah said. The truth was disorder.

Irene sat with her hand shading her eyes. "How could you do that to yourself?" she asked.

"I had to Mother," said Sarah.

"You don't realize how precious life is." Irene started to cry. "You have no right to be so reckless." She searched her pocket and pulled out a handkerchief. She wiped her eyes and put the handkerchief away.

"It's my life," Sarah said.

"Your life is a gift," Irene said.

"It doesn't feel like a gift, Mother," said Sarah. "It feels like punishment."

"Your father can't bear to even talk about this," her mother said.

Sarah pushed her chair away from the table but she didn't stand up.

"Even when you were little, you demanded more than the others. We were forced to pay more attention to you," Irene said.

Sarah didn't want to but she started to cry.

"I wanted to be fair and treat you all equally," said Irene. "We didn't want anyone to feel cheated."

"I felt cheated."

"How could you have possibly felt cheated? We gave you everything we could."

Sarah wanted to burst in the silence. She stood up and went to the window.

"Don't you ever think of anyone but yourself?" Irene asked.

She hadn't napped but she told her mother she had. It was her first lie. Laura and Peter were asleep in the same room. Irene lifted Sarah over the rail of her crib through the chilly air to the floor. Could she have a graham cracker please? Irene said she could have one now or she could have one when the others got up, but she couldn't have two. Sarah said she wanted hers now. Maybe Irene would have one herself and they could sit on the front stoop together and have a picnic. But her mother had ironing to do. She left Sarah sitting alone on the stoop with a graham cracker. Sarah remembered it as a cold afternoon, though it might have only been cloudy.

Irene pulled her handkerchief from her skirt pocket again and blew her nose. "Most people end up coming back to where they started and find what they're looking for," she said. "I pray that will happen to you."

"I'm not as good as you are," Sarah said.

"Nonsense," said Irene. "Everyone is basically good."

"Not everyone Mother," said Sarah.

"Don't ever tell your father what you just told me," her mother said. Her mouth trembled. "I don't think he could take it."

Sarah saw her father's pale face, his tight mouth. "I don't think I ever would," she said.

"I hate to cry," said Irene. She covered her nose with one hand.

"Why?" Sarah said with emotion. Seeing her mother cry had given her hope.

"Because I look ugly when I cry," said Irene.

Twenty-six

Lloyd poured vodka into Laura's glass and put the bottle back under the sink. The vodka was kept under the sink now that Myrtie lived with them.

"I bought insurance when I was a young man," he said. "Today people buy land. You're in the right business."

"Thank you," said Matthew. He stood with his arms crossed watching everything Lloyd did. Sarah looked at Matthew's blue eyes, his excellent color.

"The first profit I made was on a little house we fixed up," Lloyd said. "It didn't have electricity or running water."

Sarah remembered a photograph of her mother pregnant in front of some shack.

"Eventually I built your mother the house she wanted," said Lloyd.

"Her dream house," said Laura. She looked at Matthew.

"We had a plan," Lloyd said. "You have to have a plan."

"Did everything go according to plan?" Matthew asked.

"No one expected the bottom to drop out of the economy the way it has," Lloyd said.

They picked up their drinks but no one drank. They stood in a circle looking at each other. Someone coughed.

"People think tomorrow will never come," Lloyd said. "But it does." They walked single file back into the living room.

"When you get sick over there, they give you tea and jello," Mildred was saying.

"She needs protein," said Myrtie.

"Who's sick?" Laura asked.

"Emma Cassidy has the flu," said Mildred. "She's living at Fox Ridge Manor now. It's such a nice place."

"It is a nice place," said Irene.

"I miss Margaret," said Mildred.

"I know you miss Margaret," Irene said. "But you aren't ready for Fox Ridge Manor."

"Did everybody hear that Bert Sheffick died?" Lloyd asked.

"I didn't know he died," Laura said. She sat on the couch next to Matthew. "Why didn't I know?"

"The reason I even bring it up," said Lloyd, "is that Bert Sheffick is an example of a man who didn't protect his family."

"No one thinks he's really going to die at fifty-two," said Irene.

The Shefficks were the next-door neighbors who moved

to Houston. Sarah remembered Judy and Mark as kids with no personalities. Bert Sheffick used to be on the radio. He sounded handsome but he wasn't.

"Ellie and the kids came by in October, wasn't it hon?" Lloyd said.

"Judy walked in with this thing in a velvet bag," Irene said. "It looked heavy but she wouldn't put it down. Finally I asked her, what's in the bag Judy?"

"What did she say?" Laura asked.

"She said, Dad." Irene covered her nose. "I said, pardon me? I thought I'd misunderstood. She said, Dad."

"Judy was carrying Bert's ashes around in this urn," Lloyd said. "She showed it to us. Big brass thing."

"So what did you do?" Laura asked. She looked around at everyone with her eyes big.

"She handled it just great. Tell them what you said hon."

"I said, I'm so glad he could make it."

Everybody laughed.

"I don't want to be cremated," Laura said and frowned at Matthew.

"Seriously," said Lloyd. "That girl has a problem. She's going to have to let go one of these days."

"Ellie said they'd been carrying that urn around for a month," said Irene.

"Why shouldn't they carry it around if it makes them feel better?" Sarah asked her.

"I didn't say they shouldn't," Irene said.

"I hope nobody carries me around in a jar," Myrtie said in a loud voice.

"It's an unhealthy dependency," said Lloyd.

"Maybe it isn't," said Sarah. "How do you know?"

"Anyway we got a kick out of it," said Irene. She folded her hands on her lap.

"What's wrong with you, Sister?" Lloyd asked.

"She's in a bad mood," said Laura.

"No I'm not," said Sarah.

"Tell me," Lloyd said. "Don't you think Judy ought to get on with her life?"

"I don't see that it's any of our business," Sarah said. She stood. "I don't think we ought to judge her."

Lloyd crossed his arms over his chest then he crossed his legs.

"My boys would never have talked to me that way," Myrtie said.

"He's not judging her," said Irene. "Now somebody go check the turkey."

"We'll go," Laura said.

"Why don't you leave Dad alone?" she asked Sarah in the kitchen.

"Why are you trying to protect him?" Sarah asked back. She shoved her hand into the oven mitt.

"You know how sensitive he is," Laura said in a low voice.

"Nobody tells the truth around here because somebody might get hurt," Sarah said. She opened the oven door.

Laura stood right behind her. "Hurting people is cruel."

"Either you're honest or you die," Sarah said. She lifted the tinfoil up and looked at the turkey. The turkey was brown. She let the oven door slam shut.

"Either you master yourself or you don't, is what I think," Laura said.

Sarah threw the oven mitt on the counter. It was Christmas. They were going to have to start a new year. She went out into the back hall and got her coat off the peg by the door.

"Why don't you try not to be so depressing. Try to get the holiday spirit," Laura said.

Sarah opened the door.

"Where do you think you're going? You can't just walk out on Christmas day," Laura said. "The roads are terrible."

"Merry Christmas," Sarah said when Harriet Sawyer opened her door. Sarah was used to seeing Harriet at the newspaper office. Harriet looked different at home. She looked defeated.

"It comes once a year. You get used to it," Harriet said.

"I had a fight with my dad," Sarah said on the way back to the kitchen. "And my sister." The living room was gloomy but ahead the kitchen was bright.

"Life is a series of fights," said Harriet. She turned off the television on the counter and poured Sarah a drink. "Martini," she said. Sarah had never drunk a martini before. They sat on stools at the counter. Somewhere in the house a clock struck four. Her father was probably carving the Christmas turkey.

"You must feel pretty damn good when you look in the mirror," Harriet said.

"I never feel good when I look in the mirror," said Sarah.

"I've been pondering the fact that I'm an ugly woman," Harriet said.

"You're not ugly," said Sarah.

"It's hard to believe in your own beauty when you never see it. Edward made me feel beautiful. I miss Edward."

Sarah looked out the window at Harriet's bleak yard. "Who's Edward?" she asked.

"He was a spoiled man who wanted me to take care of him the way his mother did," Harriet said. "And I did. I loved him."

"That sounds nice," Sarah said. She listened to the sounds of the house, time passing.

"We almost didn't go to Cuba. I'll always be grateful we went. It was the one important thing we did together."

Sarah wished she could go to Cuba.

"I never believed Edward when he said he loved me. I thought people probably wondered, how did she get such a handsome man?"

"Oh Harriet," Sarah said. She wanted to touch Harriet's hand.

"I would hate to be a twin," Harriet said. "I would hate to be reminded of myself all the time."

Sarah studied the grocery list taped to Harriet's refrigerator door. Cat food, vermouth, paper towels. She looked at the grease spatters on the stove. "Having a twin is like having a part of yourself out of control," she said. "A part that can betray you."

"Pretty women betray themselves. You must be strong, my dear," said Harriet.

"Am I strong enough to be strong?" Sarah asked.

"That isn't a stupid question," said Harriet. She poured two more drinks. "Don't bruise them," she told herself. She had begun to slur her words.

While they were drinking their martinis, Harriet's long-haired cat came in and rubbed against Sarah's legs. The cat was huge.

"Don't let Pumpkin up if you don't want to," said Harriet.

Sarah let him up anyway. She felt tender toward the cat.

"One thing I can tell you." Harriet rested her chin on one palm. "If I had your face I'd go into broadcasting."

Sarah saw herself as a broadcaster. She was waiting for her cue. Her makeup was perfect and she couldn't move her face. When the cue came, she couldn't talk.

"Whatever happened to the guy on the motorcycle?" Harriet asked. She looked around her kitchen as if she might redecorate it.

"He left me," Sarah said. She laid her head on her arms and closed her eyes.

"Men are always leaving," Harriet said.

Later when Harriet's cat jumped to the floor, Sarah sat up straight with her heart beating fast. She had been dreaming she was attacked by a yellow cat that climbed out of a canal. She killed it the way her Grandfather Stockman used to kill chickens for Sunday dinner. She was carrying the head along a dusty path when a lion jumped her.

Twenty-seven

The restaurant kitchen was full of steam and fluorescent light. Sarah felt mist on her face as she and Laura rushed past the dishwasher. She thought of Vern at the Fish House with his gold chain and toupee. She would never forget him. She would always feel guilty.

A man said something cordial-sounding in Chinese and everyone laughed. Laura apologized. Oriental men in white and women in street clothes were working along the shiny counters. The spring on the back door sang out as Sarah pushed the door open. It slapped shut behind them. Outside a trash bin sat against the high wooden fence across the alley. The night was freezing and black. It was snowing. They walked fast to the street.

Sarah started the car and pulled away from the curb.

Laura sat like an invalid on the passenger side. They drove past the campus and the new shopping center at the edge of town. Matthew had told Laura he was taking a client out to dinner and then they saw him walk into the Peking Duck Restaurant with some woman. He practically had his arm around her.

"Don't tell anyone about this," Laura said.

Sarah watched her sister stare at the radio light. The radio was playing so softly they could almost not hear it. Sarah recognized the look. She could feel the feeling.

Laura pulled her breath in sharply. "I have to think of what to do," she said.

Sarah turned onto the highway going west and took the curve before the river bridge at forty-five miles an hour. She let the car coast down the hill past the old dump and crossed the bridge going too fast. The highway was flat in the light ahead.

"I'm not going to get angry if that's what he wants," said Laura.

"I think you should get angry," Sarah said.

"I don't want him to know how I feel."

Sarah reached down and turned out the headlights. She kept the steering wheel straight. She never did it long enough for anything bad to happen. Sometimes she wished something bad would happen. She wanted her life to change while she drove through the dark fast.

"What the hell are you doing?" Laura cried. "Turn on the lights. Turn them on."

Light brought the hard look of the pavement racing toward them. Nothing loomed in their path. They drove five miles in silence.

"And I'm not going to sit around feeling sorry for myself either," Laura finally said.

Sarah turned left at the Hurricane Baptist Church onto a gravel road. There were no tire tracks in the fresh snow. A farmhouse lay ahead on the left. She stopped in the road and turned out the headlights. They sat in the dark and looked at the farmhouse where they had once lived. She remembered the sound of the wind. As a kid she had believed the wind was God.

"This isn't the first time something has happened," Laura said.

"Why didn't you tell me before?" Sarah asked.

"It isn't something you talk about," said Laura. "Remember the black eye I got on our honeymoon?"

"It wasn't a snorkeling mask that socked you in the face I can tell," said Sarah.

"He said I deserved it because I provoked him."

"You didn't deserve it."

"I didn't provoke him," Laura said.

The porch light went on at the farmhouse. In the distance the snow fell more gently.

"About a month ago I stopped by his brother's apartment on their poker night. I thought it would be fun to surprise Matthew. You know."

Laura looked at the windshield. Sarah looked at Laura's reflection in the windshield.

"Matthew and that girl were standing outside. He had on

his new ski parka and he was holding her. He never holds me," Laura said.

"Oh no," said Sarah.

"I'm sure she's a nice person," Laura said quickly. "She probably doesn't have any idea what she's doing."

Sarah closed her eyes and stopped feeling anything.

"I sat in the car praying they wouldn't see me. I would have died if they had seen me," Laura said.

The farmhouse lights went out. Nothing was visible beyond the small pocket of light from the car radio.

After a while Laura said, "I've been thinking about someone but I don't know who. It isn't Matthew."

"I don't know the man I think about either," said Sarah.

In a motel room in Gatlinburg a long time ago, she wished she could be the woman laughing on the other side of the wall. The man with her stopped humming and their bedsprings began to squeak. Sarah listened hard. She was fifteen at the time and on a family vacation. Every moment needed the right boy to complete it.

"What do you think of Matthew?" Laura asked.

"His teeth are too big."

"Nobody tells me anything until it's too late," Laura said.

"You didn't want to hear what I thought," Sarah said. She looked out into the dark. "You just wanted to be a couple."

"He says you're brighter than I am," Laura said. "Do you think you're prettier too?"

"I never thought I was prettier," said Sarah.

The darkness seemed to close in around them.

"I just wanted to be happy," Laura said. She didn't cry. "I thought things would work out."

Sarah started the car and turned on the lights. She looked at the gas gauge. She pulled into the driveway and turned around. It had stopped snowing.

They carried the rubber plant between them out to Matthew's truck. Then they went back for the piano bench. They left his leather chair and the smoking stand. They left his novels.

"What about the piano?" Sarah said.

"I'm going to have professionals move the piano and the sofa," Laura said. "If Matthew doesn't sell them first."

"Why don't you call Dad," Sarah said. "We're going to need help."

"I don't want to call Dad."

"It's true," said Sarah. "Some things you have to do by yourself."

They carried the piano bench outside and lifted it up into the back of Matthew's truck. Sarah looked across the frozen yard. Matthew was flying to Chicago. He told everyone his mother had been hospitalized because of a stroke. The truth was she was somewhere drying out.

"What about the lawn furniture?" Sarah asked.

"His parents gave it to us, so he can have it. Come on. I want all my stuff gone when he gets home." Matthew had said he would be out of town three days.

They moved the kitchen table and chairs outside and were packing boxes of kitchen appliances when a car pulled into the driveway and sat idling. Sarah looked through the window. Matthew was getting out of a taxi. He paid the driver. After the taxi drove away, he stood in the driveway in his ski jacket and sunglasses. He looked at the furniture in the truck. He looked at the furniture in the yard.

"What's he doing home?" Sarah said.

"You can't have the television," Matthew yelled. "I bought that television before we were married."

Laura went out the back door. "You were going to give it to the Salvation Army. I paid to get it fixed," she said.

"That's my suitcase," Matthew said. He walked over and dumped the clothes in it out on the ground. "You can go ahead and take this stuff," he said. "But you aren't using my truck."

He went around to the back of the truck and started dragging things out. He threw a lamp on the ground but it didn't break. He dumped the rubber tree out onto the driveway. Dirt spilled everywhere. Laura said nothing until he tossed out a large box of shoes.

"God damn it," she said. Different colored shoes lay scattered across the snow. "What are you doing here anyway?"

"A little bird told me something was going on," said Matthew. He was breathing hard.

After everything was out of the truck, he got into the driver's seat and backed out of the driveway. He squealed the tires as he drove away.

"Doesn't he piss you off?" Sarah asked. "He acts like an adolescent."

"He always acts that way," Laura said. She sat on a kitchen chair in the yard. She looked at the garage roof. She looked at the sky.

"What are you going to do now?"

"I'm going to call Dad."

"Laura. Aren't you even hurt?"

"I'm not going to let myself feel hurt," Laura said. "I couldn't stand it if I had to feel hurt."

"Then you ought to feel angry."

"I'm not going to lower myself to his level."

"If you don't feel angry, you won't feel anything."

Twenty-eight

"The Stockmans have superiority complexes," Lloyd said.

Sarah opened the refrigerator. She looked inside.

"No we don't, Lloyd," said Irene. "We have family pride." She stirred whatever was in the pot on the stove and put the lid back on. Laura was slicing an apple by the sink.

"I guess their pride makes them cold," said Lloyd.

"You think that because you were raised in an atmosphere of high emotion," said Irene.

No one growing up in the Stockman household was allowed to laugh or cry out loud, the story went. Sarah remembered her grandfather combing her grandmother's hair on a Sunday not long before she died. Rachel Stockman could no longer speak. She was sitting at the dining room table. The curtains were dusty and there were no plants in the windows. Her hair got tangled and she cried.

"My mother's got an inferiority complex," Lloyd said. "I have it too. No, I do," he said, looking at Irene.

Laura arranged the slices of apple on a plate with cheese. "What inferiority complex?" she said. "I didn't know Grandmother had an inferiority complex." She put the plate on the kitchen table. She and Sarah were sharing their old room again. Only now, there wasn't enough closet space. Myrtie had Peter's room.

"My mother got it from her mother who was illegitimate," said Lloyd. "And I got it from her."

"I didn't know anybody was illegitimate in this family," Laura said. "Why didn't I know?"

"Nobody in my family would talk about it," Lloyd said. "If the subject came up around Mother, she turned to stone." He took a slice of apple and salted it.

"This family is more interesting than I thought," Sarah said.

"What is it the Bible says? That sin shall visit a family for four generations? I'm the third generation," said Lloyd.

"Sin is still visiting us," said Sarah.

"Irene's father wouldn't come to our wedding because he thought I wasn't good enough," said Lloyd. He sat down at the table.

"Don't be ridiculous Dad," said Laura. "I'm sure he thought you were good enough. You're good enough." She hugged him.

Sarah opened a kitchen cupboard and then she closed it.

"They didn't like me," he said.

"Everybody likes you," said Laura.

"That wasn't it, Lloyd," said Irene. "Dad thought I was too young to get married. And Mother wasn't well then. He had to stay home with her."

Sarah sat down at the kitchen table and stood up again. She opened a drawer and got out some placemats.

"After a few years they accepted me," Lloyd said. He leaned back in his chair.

"It didn't have anything to do with you," said Irene. "Even if you prefer to think it did. Dad wanted me to finish college. We were farmers during the Depression."

"How many for dinner?" Sarah asked.

"Just us four," said Irene.

"What about Grandmother?"

"She's already eaten."

"I've done just as well as anybody who got a degree," said Lloyd. "Experience is the best teacher."

"No one is arguing with you," Irene said.

"I hope I didn't pass on my inferiority complex but I probably did," said Lloyd.

"I don't think you did," said Laura.

"I think he did," said Sarah.

Irene looked at Sarah. "You do have a complex," she said.

"That sounds like an accusation," Sarah said.

"I'm just saying what I think," said Irene.

"When did you first notice my complex?" Sarah asked.

"During your freshman year in college," Irene said.

Her freshman year in college, she remembered sleeping a lot. She felt guilty all the time because she had let a boy touch her. She let him do it all the time.

"Why didn't you take me to a psychiatrist?"

"I almost did," said Irene. "But I thought you were getting over it. Maybe I should have."

"She's okay. Aren't you Sister?" Lloyd said.

For a moment Laura looked sympathetic.

"Let's talk about something else," said Irene.

"Did you like living on a farm, Mother?" Laura asked.

"I grew up there so of course I liked it," Irene said.

"Growing up on a farm could also make you hate it," said Sarah. She put the placemats on the table.

"Were you poor?" Laura asked. She ate a slice of cheese.

"It's good with apple, Sister," said Lloyd.

"She doesn't eat carbohydrates," Sarah said.

"She shouldn't avoid carbohydrates altogether," said Lloyd.

"Everybody was poor during the Depression," said Irene.

"Not everybody," said Lloyd. "But I guess my family was more fortunate than most." He got up and opened the refrigerator.

"I'm glad we didn't have to go through a depression," said Laura.

"We burned our corn in the winter. You have no idea what it's like to have to burn the corn you raised as food," said Irene.

"Did you have a horse?" Laura asked.

"We had to have horses to pull our plows," said Irene. "We had cattle and pigs too. I'll never forget the smell of the feedlot. I was afraid I carried it with me everywhere on my clothes."

"I remember when we were five," Laura said. She leaned against the kitchen counter. "I was walking out by the pear trees one day when I smelled mud pies."

"Had it just rained?" Lloyd asked.

"I thought to myself, I hope I never forget this smell when I grow up." Laura seemed to be searching for something across the room. From the look on her face, Sarah thought she couldn't find it.

"Well you see?" Irene said with optimism. "You didn't forget it."

"And the milkweed pods?" Laura asked.

"They were our pearls," said Sarah. She put the plates and silverware in a pile on the table. She went over and stared out the window.

"I don't remember much about the past though," Laura said. "Sometimes I feel like I'm just floating through life and not getting a whole lot out of it."

"Are you all right, Sister?" Lloyd asked.

"I'm okay," said Sarah.

If Jack called her again, she wouldn't say anything. She would listen to his voice and then she would hang up. If he showed up at her door, she would just look at him and then she would close the door.

Twenty-nine

A hand touched her shoulder and the pinball machine went wild. Sarah was sitting at the counter in the sandwich shop. The sandwich shop was also the bus depot. Arrivals and departures were printed in colored chalk on a blackboard above the coffeemaker.

"I want to talk to you," Matthew said behind her. She turned around. He looked good in his business suit.

"What about," she said. She looked at a spot of blood on his white collar.

"I don't want to talk here," he said. He jingled some coins in his pants pocket. She started to dig around in her purse for some change but Matthew put a quarter on the counter. "Let's go," he said.

She didn't think she should but she went with him. He

kept his hand low on her back as they walked toward the door. She watched his cowboy boots. His truck was parked out front. He got in and leaned over to unlock the door. He didn't unlock it right away but watched her through the glass for a moment.

"Do you blame her?" Sarah asked the minute she got in. She slammed the door.

"For taking everything good and leaving?" Matthew said.

Two men came out of the sandwich shop. The short one punched the other on the shoulder but not in a friendly way.

"Christ Matthew. We saw you at the Chinese restaurant with that woman," she said.

"You think you know what you're talking about but you don't."

"Laura told me about the black eye. What else did you give her?"

Matthew shrugged, penniless.

Sarah looked at the sky. The sun had broken through the clouds. She looked at *Daily Courier* in gold on the window across the street.

"You've always acted like you wanted something from me," Matthew said.

Sarah looked at him. "What could I possibly want from you?"

Matthew started the engine and pulled away from the curb.

"Where are you taking me?" she said.

She opened the door when he stopped at the light but she didn't get out.

"Shut the door," he said.

She shut the door. Matthew accelerated through the intersection.

"Would you go to bed with me if I asked?" he said.

"Don't be ridiculous," she said feeling calm.

Matthew drove up the main street and turned right onto Cedar. Cedar was a street where old people lived. He pulled to the curb and parked.

"What is this all about," Sarah said. "You should be talking to Laura, not me."

"Why didn't you want me to marry Laura?" he whispered.

"I never trusted you," she said. "You don't have a sense of humor."

"You don't think I have a sense of humor?" Matthew said.

He touched her shoulder then grabbed her arm and pulled her to him. He kissed her hard. Sarah pulled away. She put her hand over her mouth.

"You want to fuck me, don't you? You've always wanted to fuck me," he said.

Sarah hit him on the head. She hit him on the shoulder. He grabbed her wrists and kissed her throat. She started to cry.

"Cry," he said. "Cry for all the times you wanted to and didn't."

She had heard this before. Stanley said it to her the night they spent in the Murphy bed. "If you weren't going to do it, why did you get into bed with me in the first place?" he asked. He sounded so disgusted, she started to cry. Then

Stanley said, "Cry for all the times you wanted to and didn't." She let him hold her and tried to cry harder.

"This is how you treated Laura," she said to Matthew. "Now I understand." She got out of the truck and slammed the door. She started walking fast.

Matthew followed her up the street in his truck tooting the horn, but she didn't turn around.

Thirty

"There's a lot of dust back here, Mildred," Lloyd said on his hands and knees. His voice came from behind the refrigerator.

"Now you know what a lazy housekeeper I am. Dust isn't dangerous, is it?" Mildred said.

Sarah held the flashlight for her father. She aimed the beam of light on his hands.

"It's combustible," said Lloyd.

"Oh my goodness," said Mildred. She sat on the church pew at the kitchen table.

"To your right Sister," Lloyd said. "Lower. Lower still. I can't see anything the way you're pointing the light."

"When the engine starts up, it goes like this," said Mildred. She made a high-pitched noise.

"Hand me the flashlight Sister so I can shine it where I need it."

"I can do it Dad. Just tell me where."

"You're at the wrong angle."

Sarah handed him the flashlight. Mildred came closer, her hands clasped over her stomach.

"Mildred." Lloyd sat back on his heels. "Can you move back a couple of feet? Your shadow falls right where I'm trying to see."

"Why don't I bring in the floor lamp if he can't see," Mildred said.

"Gad. This thing is so old, I'd just replace it," Lloyd said. "You know what you ought to do. You ought to buy one of those apartment-sized models they have at Monkey Wards." He got up and shoved the refrigerator back against the wall.

"They have a wide range of colors," said Sarah. "Avocado would be nice." She sat on the church pew she felt so bored. Her life was escaping.

"I would have a foot left over on either side of a small one," said Mildred.

"No you wouldn't," said Lloyd. "You might have two inches but not a foot."

"I want a full-sized refrigerator. I might need the space someday," said Mildred.

"I've done just about all I can," said Lloyd. He pulled a red bandanna out of his hip pocket and wiped his forehead.

"What's going on?" Laura said, coming in the back door.

"A little problem with the refrigerator," Sarah said.

"I saw some cute apartment-sized refrigerators at Monkey Wards," said Laura. "They have different colors. Avocado would look nice."

"I suppose I could go to Montgomery Wards and pick out a new one," Mildred said. She buttoned and unbuttoned her top button.

"I'll go with you," Laura said.

The back door opened and Veachel walked in. "What's this. Grand Central Station?" he said.

"A little problem with the refrigerator," Laura said.

Sarah held her chin in one hand. Maybe she could go crazy. It would be someplace to go. Someone to be.

"Lloyd thinks I should replace it," said Mildred.

"If it were mine, I'd have a look at it to see if it could be fixed," Veachel said. He rubbed the back of his neck.

"What's going on," Vera said. She pushed the back door open but didn't come in.

"A little problem with the refrigerator," said Veachel.

"Did you tell them what to do?" she asked.

The delivery men had just left. It was eight o'clock at night.

"I was taken with the color," Mildred said.

Lloyd, Irene, and Sarah were the only ones there with her. Everybody stared at the pink refrigerator.

"I knew it wasn't the size I wanted but I let him talk me into it. You'd think I would know better at my age."

"Talking people into things is what a salesman does," said Lloyd. He looked at Sarah.

"It's only a size smaller than her old refrigerator," Sarah said.

"I wouldn't have noticed if you hadn't told me," said Irene. She stepped out of one high heel and was shorter.

"I can't live with this refrigerator. The first thing tomorrow morning I'm going to see if they'll come get it," said Mildred. "I suppose I'll have to pay extra delivery charges. Those men have moved it twice already."

"Delivering appliances is their job," said Lloyd.

"For heaven's sake don't worry about that," Irene said.

"If I could, I'd call them right now. I'm going to worry about it all night," said Mildred. "I can't help it."

"Try to think about something else," said Irene.

"Who's the manager over there?" Lloyd asked. "I'll give him a call."

"What good would that do?" Irene said. She took off an earring and rubbed her earlobe.

"What do you think Veachel would advise?" Mildred asked.

Lloyd put his hands in his pockets. "I already gave you my best advice," he said.

"I'm not saying it's your fault," Mildred said. She took a Kleenex out of her sweater pocket.

"It certainly is not his fault," Irene said.

Sarah laughed but not because anything was funny. She was standing between her parents and she felt like a kid.

Sarah was holding the flashlight for her father. They had come over to hook up Mildred's new dishwasher while she was at the doctor's. Lloyd said it was easier to do it when no one was home. Sarah looked around the kitchen. Maybe wallpaper was the answer.

"To your right," Lloyd said. "A little lower."

She had decided to paint the parlor salmon, the library celery, and the dining room eggshell. She felt lighthearted about her decision to redecorate Aunt Mildred's rooms for her.

"Pay attention to what you're doing Sister," Lloyd said.

"Are you about done?" she asked.

"I took time out of my own schedule to come over here and do this," he said. "I can't tell which wire goes where. They all look the same color."

"Shit," she said.

"We'll get her here in a minute," he said.

Sarah held the light steady for a long time. The shoe factory whistle went off in the distance. It was a depressing sound.

"I'm going to have to come back and finish this some other time," he said. As he stood up the phone rang. Sarah answered it. No one seemed to be at the other end for a moment. Then she heard Jack's voice. She stared at her father.

"What do you want?" she said. She couldn't remember Jack's face.

"A man set this woman on fire," he said. "She held the flames in her arms and satisfied went back home, where she was devoured."

"What?" she said.

"You heard what I said."

"How did you find me?" Sarah said remembering his mouth.

"I told your sister I was a friend of yours. I said I had one arm. You must have really liked the one-armed guy. Your sister was very cooperative."

"He was nice to me," Sarah said.

"Hang up the phone," said Lloyd.

"I know we've had some problems but we can straighten them out," Jack said in her ear.

"Don't ever call me again," Sarah said but she couldn't hang up. She had remembered his eyes.

"I know you better than you think," he said. "You don't mean that."

"I signed a peace warrant against you," Sarah said. "You can't come inside the city limits." Lloyd had taken her down to the police station and helped her fill out the papers.

"You dumb cunt," said Jack. "Don't tell me what I can't do." He hung up.

"Is he threatening you?" Lloyd said. "If he is, I can handle it."

Sarah hung up. She felt scared. "He was testing me, Dad."

"Is this thing over once and for all?"

"Yes Dad," Sarah said.

"You just about killed your mother with this little episode," Lloyd said.

Sarah looked at him. "Is that what you call it?" she asked.

"I just want you kids to get straightened out. That's all," he said. "You try to do the right thing all your life and things get fouled up anyway. Dad gum it."

"You sound like we did something terrible to you."

"First Peter runs off, then your sister marries that jackleg, and now you're in a mess. I busted my butt for you kids for years but what I think doesn't count." Lloyd shook his head.

"Peter's a conscientious objector, Dad," said Sarah.

"I was scheduled to fly on a suicide mission to Yap Island at the end of the war," Lloyd said.

"Why would anyone go on a suicide mission?"

"We didn't question it. That's the point. I even wrote your mother a farewell letter."

"Oh no."

"The war in the Pacific ended and we didn't go to Yap. But it would never have occurred to me to run out on my country."

"Let's not talk about the war, Dad," Sarah said feeling miserable.

"What got to me was that he never talked it over with me. Your brother keeps everything to himself. You can't save a man from himself," said Lloyd.

"Everybody's always trying to save somebody in this family. It's a problem," said Sarah.

"There have been times I've wanted to leave everything," Lloyd said. "No really. I have a dream where I'm walking off toward the mountains leading a burro packed with supplies. Your sister thinks it's a terrible dream because your mother isn't in it. But it helps when I get under a lot of pressure. I sit back and watch myself go off with that burro and I feel better."

"My dreams don't work that way," said Sarah.

Lloyd sighed. "We just want you kids to be happy," he said. "Don't ever tell Laura this but your mother and I were relieved when Matthew showed what kind of a person he is. We never really liked the boy, but we didn't want to interfere. He did us all a favor. He proved himself to be a real ass."

"I agree," Sarah said.

"Let me ask you one thing. What were you thinking, running off with that lowlife?"

With Jack there had been no safety and no plan. They'd had only the next day like an empty space to fall into. The freedom had felt like anger.

"Don't cry," Lloyd said, pulling his handkerchief out of his back pocket. "It isn't anything to cry about."

"Yes it is," Sarah said.

Sometimes she wanted them to forgive her and sometimes she didn't.

"It's already in the past," Lloyd said.

"Then why don't I feel forgiven?"

"If you ask God to forgive you, He will. Then you will feel forgiven."

Thirty-one

Mildred wore white gloves and a hat. She held on to Sarah's arm with one hand and carried her pocketbook with the other.

"Who cut your hair?" Sarah asked. She smelled food and then a cart of dinner trays rolled by in the corridor.

"Marsha Stewart cut it," Mildred said. Right after Lloyd got the new dishwasher hooked up, she told them she wasn't going to go on living in that big old house alone. She said she intended to live at Fox Ridge Manor with her friend Emma Cassidy.

"Marsha was a year behind you girls in school," she said. "Her brother used to deliver our groceries. He was such a well-mannered boy. You have to make an appointment with her two days in advance."

"You don't look like yourself in short hair," Sarah said.

"Vera said it would be easier to take care of short hair," said Mildred. She started to button her sweater.

"Are you cold?"

"I've worn this sweater every day since Margaret died," Mildred said.

"Do you ever get warm?"

"No. I never do," said Mildred.

"Where's your shawl?"

"I wouldn't want to wear a shawl and a sweater both. Hello Maureen. This is my great-niece who takes pictures for the *County News*." Sarah had a new job. It was okay.

The woman clutched her hand to her mouth and nodded as they passed. She had no eyebrows. Her eyes looked terrified.

"This is my great-niece who works for the county newspaper," Mildred said to a man with a walker. "She used to work for the city paper but she decided to branch out."

"It's good to get out into the county," said the man.

"William Trott," Mildred said to Sarah. "He used to own the feed store in Beulah."

"He has beautiful hair," Sarah said.

"All the Trotts have full heads of hair. Did you sleep last night, Ethel?" Mildred said to a woman sitting in the hall. "Ethel doesn't sleep." Mildred patted her hands. They lay in a knot on the blanket over her lap. The hands did not move.

"Good afternoon to you, Wilma," Mildred said to the woman in the room behind Ethel. All the rooms looked out onto a small flagstone courtyard. In the courtyard it was raining.

"You seem to know everyone," Sarah said.

Mildred pulled her close. "I'm one of the ones who can get around," she said. "I do what I can. Some of them don't know anything."

They walked on down the hall toward a small woman in a wheelchair. Two women walked out of a room crying.

"Millicent, I want you to meet my great-niece who works for the county newspaper," said Mildred. "Her twin sister works at the hospital. I expect she'll be head nurse over there before long."

"Why doesn't she come work here?" Millicent asked.

"A lot of people can't tell them apart," said Mildred. "I've never had any trouble."

"Now what's the other one's name?" Millicent asked.

"Laura," Mildred said leaning forward. "Sarah and Laura."

"Nora?"

"No. Laura. Laura is the one with the mole on her arm," said Mildred.

"I see," said Millicent.

"We're on our way to the sunroom," Mildred said.

"There isn't any sun today," Millicent said behind them.

"There's always sun whether you can see it or not," Mildred said. "I saw those pictures you took of the solar eclipse," she told Sarah.

"I didn't take them, Aunt Mildred. They were UPI photos from Mexico. Indian women living in the mountains held candles during the darkness to ward off evil."

"There won't be another eclipse before the year two thousand and I won't be around to see it," said Mildred.

They entered a man's room. He shrugged his good

shoulder and made kissing sounds. "Edwin? You remember me telling you about my nieces. Yes you do. I sat right there on your bed one afternoon and told you all about them," Mildred said.

"Nice to meet you," Sarah said.

Mildred went to his bulletin board and took down a picture of a little girl. Edwin made more kissing sounds. Tears came to his eyes. "This is his little angel," Mildred said. She showed the snapshot to Sarah then she put it back on the bulletin board.

"Aren't you glad we don't have to get out in it?" she asked in the sunroom. She looked out at the rain.

"Maudie, Maudie," a thin voice cried up the hall.

"We'll stop and see Emma Cassidy on the way back," she said. "Her grandson went to Salt Lake City and became a Mormon."

"Frank a Mormon?" Sarah said.

"Emma's brother lives in the north wing. He has trouble with his feet."

Sarah looked at the drizzle on the window. She had imagined that Mildred would need her.

"Louise Beckman has been to see me three times. Her daughter brings her. They have a big Oldsmobile. Her son-in-law is a dentist."

"Why do you want to live here?" Sarah asked.

"What else am I going to do at my age?"

"You can take care of yourself," Sarah said. "You don't need this."

"I'm better off here with Emma Cassidy. Emma needs me," said Mildred. "That big old house was too much for me anyway. You girls ought to go live in it."

Sarah stood and walked to the window. She touched the cold glass.

"Where did you disappear to?" Mildred asked. "Nobody would tell me."

"I went up to Canada and then I was in Michigan."

"I just wanted to know," Mildred said. "Something like that happened to me a long time ago."

"Was that when you went to the Rockies?" Sarah asked.

"Yes it was," said Mildred. "I went by train with Emma Cassidy to visit her cousins."

"I went away with a man," Sarah said.

"I think I knew that," said Mildred. "Just so you didn't get hurt."

"Probably no one else would want the experience I had," Sarah said, "but it's mine."

Mildred took a small leather book out of her purse. "I've been saving this for you," she said. "It was Margaret's."

Sarah took it but she didn't open it right away. Then she opened it.

March 1. It rained and drizzled today. Myrtie is sick with flu. So far Lloyd hasn't taken the mumps. Veachel was okay and going to school yesterday. I worked most all day on the quilt pieces. Mildred spent the day with Emma Cassidy. I just listened to Amos and Andy. I am feeding the lamb and then going to bed.

March 2. This morning dawned beautiful not a cloud to be seen. Lindbergh's baby was kidnapped last night. So far no trace has been found of it. Vivian came up and listened to the radio. I corded wood and am all tired out. Lloyd is taking the mumps and Ansel isn't feeling good.

March 3. It's been a damp cold day. Still no clue to the missing Lindbergh baby. No mail today. Mildred went and sat with Emma

Cassidy again today. Some people think more of their friends than they do their sister.

March 4. I worked at the quilt again. We heard today that Arnold Lerner shot and killed his wife, her son, and then killed himself last night. I remember him as a small boy when we were growing up. Vivian came over and stayed till ten-thirty. Then I fed the lamb. It drank all of its milk this time.

March 5. It turned so cold this a.m. and snowed and blowed to beat the band. I dressed a hen for our Sunday dinner. I sat up alone and kept the fire going so my fruit upstairs won't freeze.

March 6. It was two above zero this a.m. I didn't lose anything and we had our chicken. It was so good but not like it would have been if the children would have been here to help eat it. Myrtie has the flu and Lloyd has the mumps.

March 8. The little chickens are hatching. I received letters from Alvin and Bernice Woods and Sybil Stinson.

March 9. This is Ansel's fortieth birthday. I wish they were here tonight. The little lamb is sick. Has been sick all day. Matilda Willers is not expected to live through the night. Mr. Cassidy and Mr. Gustin were both here today about the wood. We have thirty-two little baby chickens upstairs tonight. I hope I may raise every one of them.

March 10. Still very cold. Matilda is still very sick. The little lamb died this a.m.

Sarah hoped Margaret was holding the lamb when it died. She didn't want Margaret to be lonely. She put her hand out where Mildred could touch it. Mildred touched it.

"I suppose she wrote some things in here that she didn't want me to know," Mildred said and showed Sarah where some pages had been torn out of the back.

"She just wanted some privacy, Aunt Mildred," Sarah said. "It wasn't anything personal." She looked at her great-aunt's face. She looked all around it. "I can't get used to you with short hair," she said.

"I wouldn't let them clip my neck," Mildred said. She touched the back of her neck. "Veachel clips Vera's neck."

Thirty-two

Sarah looked at the light coming in through the window. Outside the day was bright but the curtains kept the room dim. She and Laura were sitting on the hardwood floor in the library of their great-aunts' house, sorting through boxes of photographs.

After his daughters moved into Margaret's and Mildred's house, Lloyd came over and took up all the old carpeting. "Those beautiful wood floors hidden all these years," Irene said when she saw them.

Sarah pulled out a photograph of herself and Laura in a wheelbarrow. They were wearing identical winter coats and bonnets. Myrtie stood by the wheelbarrow in a fur coat with large, square shoulders. Her expression was pained. Irene said the picture was taken about the time her mother-in-law started putting on weight.

"Which one is me?" Laura asked. "I always forget."

"The one on the left," Sarah said. The child on the left looked more alert.

Laura held up a snapshot. "Who is this man?" she asked.

In the snapshot Mildred wore a summer dress and white gloves. She held a hat on with one hand. The brim cast her face in shadow. A man in a white suit and a small mustache stood beside her on the balcony. In the distance were some mountains.

"This was Mildred's trip to the Rocky Mountains," said Sarah. "That man must be Emma Cassidy's cousin."

"I didn't know Aunt Mildred had a boyfriend," Laura said. "Why didn't she stay in Colorado?"

"Maybe she didn't love him enough. Maybe he didn't love her," said Sarah. "People come home for a lot of reasons."

"If ever I got to Colorado, I wouldn't come home. You don't suppose she came home because of Margaret."

Sarah remembered Mildred and Margaret walking downtown on the square one day. They wore identical navy blue dresses and carried purses on their left arms. They crossed the street in step. The only difference between them was Mildred's glasses.

"How do you feel when we're together?" she asked.

Laura hesitated. "I have always felt that nothing is missing when we're together," she said. "I wanted that feeling with Matthew but it never happened."

"Do you feel like half a person when we're apart?" Sarah asked.

"No," Laura said and laughed. "Do you?"

Sarah remembered herself and Laura walking down a sidewalk together in tailored coats. They were on their way to psychology class. Some boys turned to stare at them and as Laura's shoulder touched hers, she felt whole. She felt the safety of their isolation. Now she felt the danger.

"Remember the truck pulling away without me at your wedding?" Sarah asked.

"I never said anything to Stanley about that but I wish I had," Laura said. "He was driving like a madman. Somebody could have gotten hurt."

"I shouldn't have gotten on."

"Of course you should have gotten on," Laura said.

"Your wedding had nothing to do with me," Sarah said, "but I felt that it did."

"It had something to do with you. You were my maid-of-honor," Laura said.

Sarah got up and walked to the window. She stared out for a moment and said, "I feel obligated to live with you because you're alone. But your divorce doesn't have anything to do with me either."

Laura looked at her. "I don't want anyone feeling sorry for me," she said. "That would be an insult."

"Maybe we shouldn't live together," Sarah said.

"I knew this would happen," Laura said. "I knew you would back out. What's wrong with living here until you get your feet back on the ground? You've just been through a rotten time yourself."

"I want to live alone," said Sarah. She studied the winter afternoon.

"You want to be alone too much. It isn't normal to be alone all the time."

"When I'm alone I feel larger."

"The thing I regret most in my life is that you don't like being a twin," Laura said. "The great thing about having a twin is that you don't have to be alone."

The way Laura was sitting cross-legged on the floor, she seemed unaware of the pounding silence, the violent solitude of the room.

"Yes you do," Sarah said. "You still have to be alone."

"Something terrible is happening to our future," said Laura. "We have a chance to be close and we're wasting it."

"Maybe it isn't the time to be close," Sarah said.

"I don't understand you," Laura said.

Sarah took hold of the curtains and pulled. They came down easily. They were old and fragile and dusty. The small branches of the elm outside scratched the window like fingers trying to get in. Sunlight slipped through the moving branches into a pattern on the floor. Sarah watched the light dance in the shadows. She knelt beside Laura and watched the light struggling to be free of the pattern that held it.

Marvin's was noisy with workmen and college students. Sarah and Laura sat at the bar. The jukebox was going and people were dancing fast on the dance floor. Laura looked out at them.

"It isn't too noisy?" Sarah said. "It doesn't upset you?"

"It makes me feel less depressed," Laura said. Matthew had filed for divorce that day. She didn't take off her rabbit jacket and looked glamorous.

"What'll you girls have?" Marvin asked. He put his hand with the missing fingers on the bar.

"White wine," said Laura.

"Whiskey without ice," Sarah said unzipping her leather jacket.

"What are you thinking?" Laura said. "You look sad."

"I'm thinking about leaving town," Sarah said and felt afraid.

She had dreamed she was staying in a cheap hotel at the tip of a peninsula in France. The hotel left its doors open to the sea air. The cool lobby was filled with sunlight. She loved a man who looked like Jack. She was not afraid in her dream. He was the jazz pianist who played in the hotel bar starting at three o'clock in the afternoon. She sat at a small round table and drank whiskey without ice.

Laura dragged an enormous suitcase into the lobby and cried, "How can you do this?"

"What have I done?" Sarah cried back. Laura's voice was also inside her. To have the voice both inside and outside her was unbearable. A sob escaped one of them.

"You're leaving again," Laura said. "You leave everybody."

"I'll be back," Sarah said.

Then Irene appeared with her suitcase. She looked refreshed. She and Lloyd had been touring the French countryside. Sarah knew she wasn't the daughter Irene was looking for. They embraced with tenderness.

Sarah picked up her shot glass and drank the whiskey. She put her hand on her chest to hold in breath, life.

"I worry about you," Laura said. "You're too serious. I want you to be happy."

"Being happy isn't the most important thing in the world to me right now," Sarah said.

Laura laughed. "I know you think I'm shallow but I want to be happy."

"I know you do," Sarah said. She touched the rim of her glass. She was going to be a twin for the rest of her life.

A college student asked Laura to dance but she said no. He stood there and talked to her with his back to Sarah. A man in beige clothes and hunting boots sat down next to Sarah. He ordered a drink. Their arms touched but neither of them moved away.

Design by David Bullen
Typeset in Fournier
by Wilsted & Taylor
Printed by Haddon Craftsmen
on acid-free paper